New Again

Don Tassone

Toerner Press

Paperback ISBN 9798218651138

Cover design by Farrukh Kahn

Contents

Also by Don Tassone

Get Back

Drive

Small Bites

Sampler

New Twists

Snapshots

Francesca

Collected Stories

Musings

Journeys Within

Flash 50

Clara's Big Discovery

The Liberation of Jacob Novak: And Other Stories

For Liz

Preface

The publisher for three of my short story collections was closing. So I needed to find a way to keep these stories in circulation or risk them vanishing.

As I took a fresh look at all the stories in these collections, I thought: why not pick some favorites, add some new ones and put together a new collection?

That's what I've done. These 25 stories now have a new home. I hope you enjoy them all.

Don Tassone

Discovery

New Eyes

Betsy Mitchell heard her doorbell ring. She twitched and sunk lower in the sofa. *Could be someone selling candy bars or those Jehovah's Witnesses*, she thought.

She set her cup of tea down on a coaster on the coffee table, slowly got up from her armchair, her knees creaking, and peeked around the doorway, through the living room to the front door. Through the slim pane of leaded glass alongside the door, she could make out the figure of someone standing on the porch. The visitor tried to peer in through the sidelight. *Melinda!*

"Well, hello!" Betsy said, opening the door. "What a treat to see you here."

"Hi, Mom," Melinda said, stepping up into the foyer and giving her a hug. "Where have you been? I've been calling all afternoon."

"I'm sorry, dear. I guess I was out in the garden."

"Didn't you have your cell phone with you?"

"No, honey. I guess left it in the house."

"You really need to start carrying that cell phone with you, Mom. That's why we bought it for you, you know."

"I know, honey, and I appreciate it. I really am keeping it with me most of the time. I just happened not to bring it with me this afternoon. I'll do better."

It was a white lie. Betsy didn't want to tell her daughter the real reason she hadn't been carrying her cell phone was that she was afraid to use it. Reports about a link between cell phones and brain cancer worried her.

"Would you like something to drink?" Betsy asked, in part to change the subject.

"Sure, I'd love a Diet Coke if you have one."

"Diet Coke?" she said, as they walked into the kitchen. "Aren't you afraid of all those chemicals?"

"Not really, Mom. I think the sugar's a lot worse for you."

"Maybe you're right," Betsy said. "Would you like to sit in the family room or stay in the kitchen?"

"Let's just sit here in the kitchen," Melinda said.

"Okay. Have a seat at the table. I'll get your soft drink. By the way, why were you trying to call me this afternoon? Is everything okay?"

"Everything's fine with us," Melinda said. "I was calling to talk about you."

"Here you go," Betsy said, as she handed her daughter a glass of Diet Coke, which she reluctantly kept for guests. "Just a minute, dear. Let me get my tea."

Betsy went into the family room, retrieved the cup of herbal tea she had been drinking and sat down at the small, square, oak table next to Melinda. She had brought two coasters from the family room with her. She put one under her cup and slid the other over to Melinda.

"Okay," Betsy said, sitting down. "I'm all set now."

"Mom, I'm a little concerned about you," Melinda said, shifting in her chair. "So is Tim. You seem, well, you seem to be so afraid these days."

"What do you mean, dear?" Betsy said, sipping her tea.

"Well, I don't want to sound dramatic. But you just seem so anxious anymore and, well, so afraid of everything. Think about what you just said about my Diet Coke. It's just a soft drink, Mom. I know that's a little thing, but it seems so many things scare you these days, and you seem more and more withdrawn. You hardly ever leave the house anymore. I don't mean to barge in here and tell you how to live. But I love you, Mom, and I want you to be happy. That's all. I just want you to be happy," she said, gently placing her hand on her mother's.

Betsy had a sad look in her eyes, as if she could cry.

"I'm okay," she said, taking another sip of tea and looking away.

"Mom."

Betsy put her cup down.

"You're right," she said softly, looking at her daughter. "I am afraid. I'm afraid of a lot of things these days. But it's a scary world, and I, well, I just wish your father were here."

"I wish he were too, Mom. I miss him so much, and I can only imagine how lonely you must be. But here you are, and I'm concerned for your well-being."

"To tell you the truth, so am I," Betsy said. "My life has become heavy. I don't want it to be this way, but I don't know what to do."

"Mom, I've been talking with Tim about this and a couple of friends too. I have an idea."

"You do?"

"Yes. I have someone I'd like you to see. He's a psychiatrist. His name is Irv Schneider. I've met him socially, but I don't know him well. I have a couple of friends who see him, though. They think he's wonderful. They say he's smart, and he has a great way with people. I think you should see him. Would you be open to that, Mom?"

"If you think he can help me, yes," she said.

"Good," Melinda said, sounding relieved. "I'll be happy to make an appointment for you, if you like."

As her mother's health care power of attorney, Melinda made most of her medical appointments these days.

"Yes, dear. That would be fine."

"Good," Melinda said. "I'll try to get you in to see him next week, if that's okay."

"Yes. Where is his office?"

"It's downtown."

"Oh. How will I get there?"

Betsy hadn't driven a car in nearly two years.

"Here's what I was thinking. I drop Sophia off at pre-school at 8:00 every morning. There's a bus stop right next to her school. I could pick you up on our way to school. What would you think of taking the bus downtown after I drop her off and before I head to work? I could try to make you an appointment for mid-morning. You could see Dr. Schneider, then grab lunch somewhere and catch the bus back. I would be waiting for you at Sophia's school. What do you think? Would that be okay?"

"That sounds wonderful, honey. I'm just sorry I have to put you to so much trouble."

"It's no trouble at all, Mom. I'm just glad you're open to this. I have a feeling Dr. Schneider is going to be able to help you."

"I hope you're right," Betsy said, smiling and patting her daughter's hand.

Melinda left just before 5:00. Betsy went back into the family room and turned on the TV, just in time to catch "The Five" on Fox News. She tuned into Fox News shows nearly every evening, usually for several hours. Tonight, she decided to watch "The Five," make herself some dinner, then catch Martha MacCallum and maybe Tucker Carlson and Sean Hannity after that.

As the TV came on, there was a commercial for gold coins, "the safest way to protect your wealth in these uncertain economic times."

Ted had never made much money, and the little they'd been able to save might have to last Betsy a long time. *Maybe I should convert some of our savings to gold*, she thought. *That way, if the economy collapses and there's a run on the banks, I'll still have money.*

She grabbed a pad and a pen and was about to write down the number to call when the commercial ended. Now there was a commercial for ready-to-eat foods in case of an emergency. Images of tornadoes, floods and armed men flashed across the screen. Betsy had been worrying about her food security too. What if there were a blizzard or the country were invaded? Having some of these ready-to-eat meals on hand seemed like a good idea. This time, she wrote down the toll-free number before the commercial ended.

Now "The Five" was on. Tonight's roundtable would begin with a look at the latest murder committed by an "illegal alien" in San Francisco, a sanctuary city and home of Nancy Pelosi.

"When will the Democrats see the light and begin to help make America safe again?" asked Greg.

The panel went on to talk about the Democrats wanting to push American toward socialism, about the rise in attacks by Muslim extremists against Christians and Jews all around the world and the high murder rate in Chicago, another sanctuary city.

The story about the Muslim extremists was especially concerning to Betsy. She had heard from a neighbor that a Muslim family was looking at a house on their block. She knew most Muslims living in the US were peaceful, but she'd grown suspicious of all Muslims anyway, not knowing which of them might be extremists. What if one of her new neighbors was a member of ISIS?

By the time "The Five" was over, Betsy was shaking. She turned off the TV, went into the kitchen and put two pots of water on the stove. She was going to have pasta, organic pasta, tonight.

She diced carrots she had dug up from her garden that afternoon and slid them down the cutting board into one of the pots of water. Then she cut into thin slices several cherry tomatoes she had picked from her garden.

She would be using extra virgin olive oil, organically grown, as her sauce for the pasta tonight and topping it with the diced carrots, sliced tomatoes and romano cheese, which she would grate.

When it came to foods, "all-natural" and "organic" were Betsy's watchwords. That's the main reason she maintained a large garden. She grew all her own vegetables and ate them fresh.

Betsy poured herself a glass of filtered water from a pitcher she kept in the refrigerator. She never drank water directly from the tap anymore.

She sat at her kitchen table and ate dinner while reading a new book, a memoir called *Wholly Unraveled*. By 6:00, she was back in the family room, watching Fox. News alerts about a fouled "dirty bomb" plot in New York made her even more anxious.

She watched until 10:00, then headed upstairs to bed, where she slept between hypoallergenic sheets with an air purifier running all night. She had a nightmare about being killed by a drunk driver.

Melinda picked Betsy up in her driveway at 7:30.

"Is this airbag on?" Betsy asked.

"Yes, Mom, it is."

"You can never be too careful, you know."

Melinda backed out of the driveway and into the street.

"Watch for cars," Betsy said. "They fly by here anymore."

"I'll keep watch, Mom. You're safe with me. I've never had an accident, you know."

"I know, honey. It's just that—"

"I know, Mom. It's okay."

Betsy slipped her left hand under her left leg and gripped the handle in her arm rest with her right hand the whole way to Sophia's school. She didn't talk because she didn't want to distract Melinda. At intersections, she closed her eyes.

When they got to school, Betsy let out a loud sigh. She was so relieved to be standing on firm ground again.

She and Melinda both gave Sophia a kiss and a hug, and she ran to the door of the school with the other kids. Betsy was glad to see there were a couple of teachers standing guard.

"Well, Mom, your bus stop is right across the street," Melinda said. "Remember your appointment with Dr. Schneider is at 11:00. So you'll probably have a little time beforehand."

"I'll be fine, honey. I might grab something at Starbucks."

"That sounds good. And you'll have lunch before you head back?"

"Yes, dear. Don't worry about me. I'll see you back here about 2:30."

"Okay, Mom. I hope you have a good session with Dr. Schneider," Melinda said, giving her mother a hug.

"Me too," Betsy said.

Melinda got back in her car and drove away. Betsy waited for the walk sign, then crossed the street, looking both ways the whole time. She sat down on a bench. The bus arrived, right on time, a few minutes later.

With stops, the bus ride downtown took just under an hour. Betsy got off about a block from Dr. Schneider's office. She knew there was a Starbucks around the corner and walked there to kill time before her appointment.

"What may we make for you this morning?" the perky, tattooed young lady said from behind the counter.

"I'd like some herbal tea, please," Betsy said.

"Certainly. Any special flavor?"

"No. As long as it's organic."

"All our teas are organic, ma'am."

"That's good. Well, do you something with mint?"

"We have a honey citrus mint, but that's a green tea, so it has a little caffeine."

"No caffeine," Betsy said, shaking her head.

"How about our peach tranquility herbal tea? No caffeine."

"That sounds good," Betsy said.

As the young lady turned around to prepare the tea, Betsy thought about the peach trees her father grew in their back yard when she was growing up. She remembered one year when insects infested the trees. Her father sprayed them with a chemical, which he used every year after that. Her mother washed the peaches and assured Betsy they were fine to eat, but Betsy was always wary after that.

"Did you say that tea is organic?" she called to the young lady behind the counter.

She turned around.

"Yes. Certified."

As Betsy sat sipping her tea, the aroma of coffee hung thick in the air. She loved coffee. She used to drink it every day. But that was before a long string of bad news about the ill effects of coffee drinking, from heart problems to cancer. Betsy hadn't had a cup of coffee, or anything with caffeine, for nearly 20 years. Now surrounded by the rich, earthy fragrance of arabica beans being ground and brewed, she really missed it.

At 10:30, Betsy left and walked to Dr. Schneider's office around the corner. His office was on the second floor of a tall office building. She went into the lobby and looked for a door for the stairs. She preferred taking the stairs over riding in an elevator. She was afraid the elevator would break down and she would be stuck between floors. She'd also seen a movie years ago where the elevator cable snapped, sending the car crashing into the basement. Since then, unless she had to go more than five floors, she always took the stairs.

Betsy found Dr. Schneider's office, signed in and filled out a form. There was a large aquarium on a long table against one wall of the waiting room with many colorful, tropical fish swimming and darting around. It reminded Betsy of the ocean. She hated the ocean. She was deathly afraid of sharks and never went into the water.

She looked up at the clock. It was 10:59. She wondered if Dr. Schneider was running late. *If he's late, and I get out of here late, I might not have enough time for lunch.*

Just then, a man appeared at the doorway to the waiting room.

"Mrs. Mitchell?" he said, smiling.

He didn't look like a psychiatrist, at least not how Betsy had always pictured one. She expected him to look clinical, nerdy and frumpy. Instead, he was young — around 40, she guessed — handsome, trim and fashionably dressed.

"Yes," Betsy said, getting up and walking over to him.

"I'm Dr. Schneider."

He extended his hand, and she took it.

"It's nice to meet you," he said.

Betsy liked his easy way. He put her at ease.

"Please, come in," he said, holding the door for her.

She stepped inside and looked around. Lamps gave the room a warm glow. The floor was wood, and there was a large area rug in the center of the room. Two comfortable-looking armchairs faced each other, each with a small end table next to it.

"Please sit wherever you like," Schneider said.

"It's funny, but I thought there'd be a couch," Betsy said.

"Ah, yes," he said. "Many of my new patients say that, but I find chairs are much better for having conversations."

"I would tend to agree."

"Please take your pick," he said, gesturing toward the two armchairs.

She stepped over to the blue one and sat down. He sat in the gray one across from her. He had a small writing tablet and a pen, which he placed on the end table next to his chair.

"So shall I call you Mrs. Mitchell or Betsy?" he asked.

"I think I prefer Betsy."

"All right, Betsy. So how are you feeling?"

"Fine."

"Well, that's good. So why are you here today?"

She looked at him and smiled.

"I'm not sure," she said.

"When your daughter made this appointment for you, she said you've become fearful and that your fears have grown worse since your husband died."

"Yes, I suppose that's true," she said.

"When did your husband die?"

"About two years ago."

"I am sorry for your loss."

He reached over and picked up his pen and writing tablet.

"What do you fear, Betsy?"

She pursed her lips and breathed in through her nose.

"To be honest, doctor, just about everything anymore."

"Can you give me an example?"

She paused and thought for a moment.

"Well, this morning, when my daughter was giving me a ride to the bus stop, I was afraid."

"Of what?"

"Getting into an accident."

"Were you in a car accident this morning?"

"No, but whenever I get into a car, I think of Ted, my husband. He died in a car accident."

"So you think that because your husband died in a car accident you'll be killed in a car accident too?"

"I think it's a real possibility."

"I see," he said, jotting a note on his tablet.

"What other fears do you have, Betsy?"

"Oh, there are lots of things really."

"For instance?"

Betsy gave him a long list of examples of the things that made her anxious and fearful, from pesticides to sharks. Dr. Schneider nodded as he made notes. She kept waiting for him to say something, but he just listened, and so she kept talking, giving him more examples of the things that frightened her.

When she finished, he asked, "How long have these things made you feel fearful?"

"Well, in some cases, for as long as I can remember," she said.

"And others, more recently. I wasn't afraid to ride in cars until Ted's accident, for example."

"I see," he said. "Let me ask you something. Have you ever actually been harmed by any of the things that make you fearful?"

"No, I guess not," she said quietly. "Not really."

"Betsy, when one of these things makes you fearful, how do you feel?"

"How do I feel?"

"I mean when you think about the possibility of eating foods with pesticides, for example, how does that make you feel?"

"Anxious."

"Can you tell me what that feels like?"

"It feels awful. When I think about going outdoors without sunscreen, for example, I immediately think about getting skin cancer. I used to love going out in the sun, doctor. When I was a girl, I would play outside all day in the summer. It was one of the great joys of my life. Now the sun frightens me, and all I want to do is stay inside. I've grown to hate the sunshine, and when I think about that, I feel sad."

"I understand," he said. "Betsy, what you just shared with me is very helpful. If it's okay with you, I'd like you to give me a few other examples of the things that are causing you fear these days and what that feels like. I'm trying to get an understanding of your concerns and the effect these concerns are having on you. So if that sounds okay, please continue."

"Of course," she said.

Betsy gave Dr. Schneider half a dozen more examples and tried to describe how her fears about these things made her feel and how her feelings were affecting her everyday life. No longer driving a car, for example, or answering her phone.

The more she shared, the more Betsy realized just how dramatically her life had changed, especially since Ted died. Her life had become so insular and lonely, and she never talked about these things with anyone, especially her children, whom she did not want to burden. But just then, it felt good to share these things with Dr. Schneider. She wasn't sure if he could help her, but she was glad she had come to see him today.

She saw him glance at his watch.

"Oh, my," she said. "I've lost track of time."

"It's okay, Betsy," he said, putting his pen and writing tablet on the end table next to him. "We still have about five minutes. You've given me a lot of good information today. Thank you. In the time we have left, I thought we could talk about our next steps."

"That sounds good," she said.

"Well, first, whether we continue these sessions is entirely your choice. But I really hope we will continue."

"I do too, doctor. I'd like to see you again."

"Very good. Why don't we make another appointment for about two weeks from now?"

"Perfect."

"Great. Next time, I'd like to ask you about your family, starting with the one you grew up in. I just want to get a more complete understanding of you, of your whole story, before I offer a diagnosis and we talk about the best path forward. Does that sound okay?"

"Certainly," she said.

She liked his calm, patient manner and the way he listened. She trusted him. She had grown wary of people, wary of the world, and it felt good to trust someone.

They both stood up. As he walked her to the door, Dr. Schneider said, "Betsy, I have a favorite quote I'd like to share as food for thought for our next session. It's by Mark Twain."

"I love reading Twain," she said. "Go ahead."

"Twain wrote, 'I am an old man and have known a great many troubles, but most of them never happened.'"

She looked at him and smiled.

"Thank you, doctor," she said, extending her hand.

"Thank you, Betsy," he said, taking it. "I'll see you again in two weeks."

"I'll look forward to it," she said.

<hr>

"So how was your appointment?" Melinda asked as Betsy got into the car.

"It was great," she said.

"Great, huh?"

"Dr. Schneider is a very good listener."

"I've heard that about him. Are you going to see him again?"

"Yes, in two weeks."

"That's great, Mom. I'll be happy to give you a ride to bus again."

"I would appreciate that, and I appreciate you suggesting I see Dr. Schneider. I have a feeling he's going to be able to help me."

As they were driving down Betsy's street, she noticed a for sale sign up in her neighbor's yard, two doors down. It was the Richardsons. Phyllis and Gene had lived there for 30 years. Betsy had known them that whole time. Now their kids were grown and gone, and Gene was retired. Betsy hadn't seen Phyllis in a while. She supposed they were ready to downsize.

Maybe I should downsize. The very idea of moving out of her house filled her with trepidation, and she put the idea out of her mind.

Two weeks later, Betsy went to see Dr. Schneider again. This time, she talked about her childhood. He asked a few questions, but mainly listened and took notes.

Two weeks later, they met again. This time, Betsy talked about her own family, about raising kids, about her marriage and about Ted's tragic death. Again, Dr. Schneider mainly listened.

They met again two weeks later. This time, Betsy talked about her daily life. She talked about how small and scary her world had become and how she wished things were different.

"Different in what way?" he asked.

"I wish I were happy again," she said. "I have not felt happiness, true happiness, in a long time."

"What's keeping you from being happy, Betsy?"

"I don't know, doctor," she said with tears in her eyes. "Can you help me?"

"Here," he said, handing her a tissue.

"I'm sorry," she said, feeling embarrassed.

"It's okay," he said. "Betsy, I have so appreciated everything you've shared with me these past few sessions. Now I'd like to share my diagnosis and talk with you about a treatment plan, which we'll develop together. Does that sound okay?"

"Yes," she said, wiping her eyes. "That sounds wonderful."

"Betsy, if you'd allow me to digress for just a moment, I'd like to briefly share something from my own life."

"Of course," she said.

Dr. Schneider set aside his pen and writing tablet.

"Thank you," he said. "When I was a kid, I knew several people who were, as we said then, mentally ill. I was very close to one of them. I didn't understand why these people were the way they were. They made me uncomfortable but, at the same time, I remember wishing there was something I could do to help them. Nobody, it seemed, was helping them, and I saw the awful effects of that, close up. As I grew up, I decided I wanted to dedicate my life to helping people with mental illness. I had heard about psychiatry, and I decided to become a psychiatrist because we are *real doctors*. We can prescribe drugs, for example. And so I began practicing psychiatry, right here, about 12 years ago. I went into it with every intention of not only helping people, but fixing them, like a doctor treats an infection, for example. But what I've learned is that I can't really fix anyone. Oh, I can prescribe drugs, which are sometimes helpful. But drugs can't fix the problems I see. I don't think any drug is going to fix your problems, Betsy. Nothing I can give you or tell you is going to make you feel comfortable driving again, for example. But I do think there is a good path forward for you."

"You do?" she asked.

"Yes, I do. First, though, I'd like to share my diagnosis with you."

"Please."

"All the things you fear might happen to you, Betsy, are real. They do exist. Sadly, cars do crash, and exposure to some chemicals does cause cancer. Now, none of these things has actually happened to you, but that doesn't mean your fears are not real. They are real. They're a part of your life, and I think the first step you need to take is to accept that. Then you can begin to see how these fears are hurting you and how that hurt is being caused not by cars or pesticides or the sun, but by you, and you can then begin to let go of your suffering by letting go of your fears."

She sat listening to him and nodding her head. It all sounded so simple, but it made so much sense.

"Let me stop there for a moment, Betsy," he said. "Does it sound like I'm in the ballpark?"

"Yes, doctor," she said. "Very much so."

"Good. If that's the case, then let me suggest a simple exercise between now and our next session. Think rationally about your fears. Give them a little space. Then begin to think about your life as it actually is. Begin to think about the things and the people you appreciate in your life. Try to see them just as they are, right at that moment, right before you. Then just draw a breath."

She waited for him to say something else, to make some other recommendation. But he just looked at her. Then he smiled and raised his eyebrows, as if to say, "Well, what do you think?"

"I think I can do that, doctor," she said.

"Good. Let's plan to meet again in two weeks and, next time, let's talk about your path forward. Okay?"

"That sounds good," she said.

They got up, and he walked her to the door.

"Betsy, the first time we met, I shared a favorite quote with you. If it's okay, I'd like to share one more."

"Yes, please."

"It's by Marcel Proust. He wrote, 'The real voyage of discovery consists not in seeking new landscapes, but in having new eyes.'"

"That's beautiful," she said. "Thank you for sharing that and for helping me begin to see that."

As Melinda was driving Betsy home, Betsy noticed the for sale sign in the Richardson's front yard had changed to a sold sign.

She had meant to stop over and talk with Phyllis. She hoped they hadn't moved yet, that there would still be time to say goodbye.

The next morning, Betsy baked some chocolate brownies and brought them down to the Richardsons as a going-away gift. It was a sunny day, and she put on her wide brim straw hat to protect her face from the sun.

She walked up the steps to the Richardsons front porch and knocked softly on the door. She had an aversion to ringing doorbells. She always felt they were too loud.

The door opened, but it was not Phyllis. Instead, a small, young, Middle Eastern-looking woman wearing a head scarf was standing there.

"May I help you?" she asked in a heavy, if lovely, accent.

"Good morning," Betsy said. "I was looking for Phyllis Richardson."

"I'm sorry," said the woman. "The Richardsons have moved away, just a few days ago. We have just moved in. I am Shakila Siddiqui."

"I see," said Betsy. "My name is Betsy Mitchell. I'm your neighbor. I live two doors down."

Betsy extended her hand. Shakila took it.

"It's nice to meet you. May I call you Betsy?"

"Yes, please do."

Just then, Betsy remembered the plate of brownies she was holding.

"I made these brownies this morning," she said. "They're chocolate. I brought them down as a going-away gift for the Richardsons, but obviously I'm a little late. May I give them to you as a housewarming gift?"

"That would be lovely," Shakila said. "Thank you. My daughter, Zia, loves chocolate brownies. She's at school now, pre-school actually. But I know she will enjoy one when she gets home."

"How old is your daughter?" Betsy asked.

"She is four. Her name is Zia."

"My granddaughter is also in pre-school. Where does your daughter go to school?"

"She goes to Woodward."

"So does Sophia, my granddaughter!"

"I'll ask Zia if she knows your Sophia when she gets home."

Shakila was standing in the doorway, looking down slightly at Betsy, who was standing on the porch.

"Would you like to come in?" Shakila asked.

"Well, maybe just for a minute."

Normally, Betsy would not have been so eager to enter a stranger's house, but she was curious, and a bit concerned, about this new neighbor and thought it might be a good idea to take a quick look around.

"Let me put these brownies in the kitchen," Shakila said. "Please have a seat in the family room, if you can find one. Sorry, we are still unpacking, as you can see."

"That's quite all right."

Betsy stepped into the family room and walked over to the fireplace to check out a framed photograph on the mantle. In the picture, she saw Shakila sitting next to a good-looking, bespectacled young man on a wooden bench with the Disney castle in the background. Shakila was holding a tiny, smiling girl, dressed as a princess, on her lap.

"I see you have found my family," Shakila said as she stepped into the room.

"Is this Zia?" Betsy asked.

"Yes."

"Zia. What a lovely name. What does it mean?"

"In Pakistan, where we are from, it means light. And with Zia, it fits for she is the light in our lives."

"How beautiful," Betsy said. "And this must be your husband."

"Yes, that is Fahad."

"And you say you're from Pakistan?"

"Yes. Fahad and I came here five years ago. We lived in New Jersey. We liked it but decided it was not the best place to raise a family. We'd like to have more children. At any rate, we decided to move here because Fahad took a job teaching biochemistry at the university. We've been living in an apartment while we were looking for a house. We feel blessed to have found this place."

"I see," said Betsy. "So your husband teaches biochemistry."

"Yes. We are both biochemists by training. We met as student at university in Punjab."

Biochemists. Betsy wondered what they did with degrees in biochemistry. Germ warfare ran through her mind.

"So what brought you to the US?" she asked.

"We both had opportunities to work for pharmaceutical companies out east, helping develop new therapies for rare diseases. We really enjoyed our work, but Fahad loves teaching, and I've decided to step off my career track and be a stay-at-home mom, at least for now. We love this country and have applied for citizenship. Zia, of course, is already a citizen."

"Well, I'm glad you're here," Betsy said.

"What about you, Betsy? Do you have a family?"

"Yes, we have three children, all grown, and one granddaughter, so far."

"And your children? Do they all live nearby?"

"No, only our daughter Melinda lives here," Betsy said with a forced smile.

"Let's have a seat," Shakila said, sitting down in an armchair and extending her hand toward the sofa.

"Thank you," Betsy said, sitting down. "Our other daughter, Jessica, lives in California, and our son, Josh, lives in New York. They're both married, but they don't have children just yet. I see

Melinda pretty often, but I don't see Jessica or Josh nearly as often as I'd like."

"I see. And how about your husband?"

Betsy looked at her and blinked.

"Ted died two years ago in a traffic accident."

"I'm sorry."

"Thank you."

The two of them sat there for a moment, looking at one another, saying nothing, as if they were both at a loss for words.

Finally, Shakila said, "Would you like something to drink? I meant to ask you earlier."

"No, thank you," Betsy said. "I really must be going. Again, welcome to the neighborhood. I look forward to meeting Zia and Fahad. Thank you for your hospitality."

Betsy went back home and made lunch for herself. Then she slathered sunscreen over her face, neck and arms, put her wide brim hat back on and headed out to her garden.

She worked there, weeding, picking vegetables and taking breaks for lemonade, sitting on a bench, for a couple of hours. As she worked, she thought about what Dr. Schneider had told her the day before, how he had urged her to sit with her fears. She thought about Shakila's head scarf. She wondered why she wore it. The very idea of it made Betsy suspicious.

She heard the high-pitched screech of a school bus braking on her street and the happy sound of children's voices. She thought of her own children coming home from school. That seemed so long ago.

She went in the house, washed up and took a little nap on her family room sofa. When she awoke, she was hungry and made herself a dinner of vegetables from her garden over organic brown rice.

After dinner, she went into the family room and turned on the

TV, just in time for Fox News at 6:00. The lead story was about a bombing at a mosque in Minneapolis. Eighteen men, women and children were killed during a religious service there.

A composite photo of their faces was shown on the screen. As she looked at all these faces, Betsy thought of the photos she had seen of Shakila, Fahad and Zia that afternoon. Their faces looked just like those on the screen. Most of the women were wearing head scarves just like Shakila's.

Then she thought about the Siddiquis as they might be at that moment. Maybe they too were learning of this terrible news. She wondered how immigrants like them deal with such a tragedy. She wondered if they feel threatened here in the US. She wondered if they feel unsafe every day, if Shakila had felt anxious when Betsy came to her front door that morning.

The bombing in Minneapolis dominated the news the rest of the evening. In addition to reports from the scene, Fox featured various experts offering running commentary on the tragedy. Most were sympathetic to the victims. But some took the opportunity to express dismay over Muslim leaders, especially the imams, not speaking out more forcefully against violence committed by Muslim extremists.

"For every action, there is a reaction," one commentator said. "It's sad to say, but maybe the members of this mosque should have seen this coming."

The very idea made Betsy feel sick. She picked up the remote and clicked off the TV, but she could not get the faces of the victims out of her mind.

She sat there on the sofa and thought of all the lives that would be changed forever as a result of the bombing that morning. She wondered if Shakila and Fahad were putting Zia to bed right now, just a few hundred feet away. She wondered if Zia knew anything about the tragedy. She hoped not. But certainly Shakila and Fahad were aware. How afraid they must be, for their daughter and themselves, on a day like this.

And she began to weep. She wept for the victims of the bombing and their loved ones. She wept for the Siddiquis. She wept for the loss of her beloved husband and how he had left her a note before going to pick up dinner for them that evening, a note which, as usual, said "I love you" and for how bad she still felt for not having had a chance to say "I love you" in return. She wept that she had not seen Jessica and Josh since Christmas, knowing it was her fault because of her fear of flying and even riding in a car.

She remembered kissing her children good night when they were little. She remembered Ted kissing her good night. She remembered her mother and father kissing her good night when she was a child and the feel of her mother's soft lips on her cheek and her father's whiskers on her neck. How grateful she was for having known these things in her life and to remember them just now.

And she remembered the flannel pillowcase on her pillow in bed when she was a girl. She loved the warm, soft feel of it on her face. How she missed that caress.

Betsy wiped away her tears and got up. She went into the kitchen and poured herself a glass of white wine, organic and sulfite-free. Then she went to her patio door, slid it open and stepped out onto her deck.

She had not been out here at night in a long time. She sat down in an Adirondack chair, which had been Ted's favorite, and looked up at the stars. It was a clear night, and the sky was filled with stars. She and Ted used to sit out here looking up at the stars all the time. He knew all the constellations and tried to teach them to her, but Betsy could never quite see them as he did.

Except for the North star, which she was always able to see. Now she looked up, and there it was, brilliant, large and luminous as ever, like a small sun, lighting up the darkness all around it. How blessed she felt, just then, to behold such a light. Light. No wonder Shakila and Fahad had named their daughter after it.

She finished her wine, went inside and turned out the lights on the first floor. She went upstairs. At the top of stairs, she turned on the light and opened the linen closet. She reached up to the top shelf and pulled down a flannel pillow case. She took it to her bedroom, took the hypoallergenic pillowcase off her bed pillow and replaced it with the flannel one. She went into the bathroom, brushed her teeth and got into bed.

The flannel felt so soft on her face. It made her think of her childhood and how safe she felt in her own bed at night. She said a prayer that Zia was feeling safe in her bed tonight, then she drifted off to sleep.

The next morning, Betsy decided to take a walk. She and Ted used to walk down the sidewalks of their neighborhood. Betsy hadn't taken many walks lately, but this morning, for some reason, she decided it might be time to start walking again.

She slathered her skin with sunscreen, put on her straw hat and headed out. She decided to turn right, past the Siddiqui's new house. As she did, she saw Shakila out in the front yard with a little girl. *This must be Zia.* They were kicking a large, plastic, bright blue ball back and forth.

Shakila spotted Betsy coming their way.

"Good morning, Betsy!" she called, having just kicked the ball to Zia.

"Good morning!" Betsy called back.

The little girl looked up at Betsy. As she did, the ball rolled by her. It rolled across the grass and over the sidewalk and between two cars parked on the street.

"Zia!" Shakila yelled.

But the girl ran after the ball. She ran across the sidewalk just ahead of where Betsy was standing and started to step between the two cars.

"Zia!" Shakila screamed, running toward her.

Betsy heard a car coming. With the speed of a much younger woman, she ran to catch Zia between the cars. She grabbed the little girl's T-shirt just as she was squeezing through and pulled her back. Betsy fell backward, landing on the grass, with Zia tumbling on top of her.

By now, Shakila had reached them. She was crying and speaking in a language Betsy did not understand. She fell to her knees, grabbed Zia and held her tightly. She looked over at Betsy, sobbing, with a mix of terror and relief in her eyes.

Betsy picked up her hat, which had fallen off, and got up.

"Is she okay?" she asked Shakila.

But Shakila didn't answer. Instead, she picked up her little girl and, still sobbing, carried her into the house and shut the door behind them.

Betsy brushed off her T-shirt and jeans, put her hat back on and resumed her walk. She walked around the neighborhood for about half an hour, thinking about Zia and Shakila and how grateful she felt to have been there for Zia at just the right moment.

Returning home, Betsy walked by the Siddiqui's house. A small SUV was now parked in the driveway, but there was no sign of Shakila or Zia.

Betsy walked on to her house and went inside. She was hungry and decided to fix herself some lunch. Today she would have an egg salad sandwich. She had made the egg salad from organic, cage-free eggs.

She was spreading egg salad on a slice of organic, whole wheat bread when she head a knock at her front door. She peaked though the living room and, through the sidelight, saw someone standing on the front porch. She could see the person was wearing a head scarf and realized it was Shakila.

She wiped her hands, went to the door and opened it.

"Well, hello, Shakila," Betsy said.

"Hello, Betsy," she said, smiling. "I brought you these," she said, handing her a bouquet of flowers. "Thank you for saving Zia this morning. Thank you for my daughter."

Betsy looked at Shakila, who had tears in her eyes. In that moment, she reminded Betsy of Melinda and, without knowing whether it was acceptable to embrace in the Muslim culture, she opened her arms and embraced Shakila, as she would her own daughter. The two women stood there for a moment, holding each other.

"Is Zia okay?" Betsy asked.

"Yes, she is fine," Shakila said, wiping away her tears. "She is taking a nap. Fahad is home with her now."

"I'm glad," Betsy said. "Would you like to come in? I was just making lunch. Would you like to join me?"

"I would love that," Shakila said, "if it's not too much trouble."

"No trouble at all."

They walked into the kitchen.

"I was just making myself an egg salad sandwich," Betsy said. "Would you like one?"

"That sounds delicious," Shakila said. "My mother used to make egg salad all the time."

"She did?"

"Yes, I grew up on a farm. My parents raised chickens. We always had eggs."

"I see," said Betsy. "Well, I hope you enjoy my egg salad. It's made from cage-free eggs."

Shakila smiled.

"Our eggs were anything but cage-free. We kept our chickens in a coop to keep them safe."

"That makes sense," Betsy said.

"Do you ever use paprika in your egg salad?" Shakila asked.

"No, but I have paprika. Would you like me to add some?"

"I'd love that, if you think you'd like it," Shakila said.

"Well, I've never tried it in egg salad, but I'll give it a try," Betsy said.

She stepped over to a spice rack on the counter.

"All my spices are certified organic," she said, picking out a small glass jar of paprika.

"We used to make paprika from chili peppers we grew on our farm," Shakila said. "It's a wonderful spice. I use it in my cooking all the time."

"Who knows?" Betsy said. "Maybe this paprika is from Pakistan."

Shakila laughed.

"Maybe so," she said. "Maybe it came from our farm."

"Would you like something to drink?" Betsy asked.

"I'd love some coffee, if you have it."

Betsy gave her a quizzical look.

Shakila smiled.

"Yes, I know. You might not expect someone from Pakistan to like coffee. But ever since we came to America, I've loved it. I drink coffee every day."

"Well, I don't make it very much anymore. But I keep some in the freezer. It's good stuff, from Colombia, I think."

"Sounds wonderful," Shakila said.

Betsy went to her freezer and pulled out the bag of coffee. It was already ground. She put a filter in her coffee maker and poured in enough coffee for two cups. She poured two cups of water into the machine and turned it on.

Soon, the aroma of coffee filled the air. It smelled so good to Betsy.

She took two white coffee mugs out of her cupboard and sat them on the counter. When the coffee was finished brewing, she poured it into the mugs.

"Would you like cream or sugar?" she asked.

"No, thank you," Shakila said. "Just black."

"Me too," Betsy said, bringing their coffee mugs over to the kitchen table and setting them down.

The two women sat down to eat. Betsy picked up her coffee mug. She held it under her nose, closed her eyes and breathed in the warm, earthy aroma. It smelled so good. She opened her eyes, brought the mug to her lips and sipped the hot coffee. She had almost forgotten how much she loved the taste of it.

"It's delicious," Shakila said.

Betsy looked at her across the table. In that moment, she saw Shakila not as a stranger or a friend or a Muslim. She saw her as a mother, as if with new eyes, and she felt a sense of peace, a wholeness, she had not known for a long time.

"By the way," Shakila said. "I asked Zia about your Sophia. As it turns out, they are in the same class together."

Betsy smiled.

"It's a small world," she said.

"It is indeed," Shakila said, biting into her egg salad sandwich.

The Old House

No sooner had Bob retired when he learned his old house, the house he'd grown up in, was on the market.

Bob was thrilled. He had always been nostalgic, and he loved that house. It held such precious memories. Now he might actually own it! He could easily afford it. His wife wasn't crazy about the idea but also said she wouldn't stand in the way.

Bob went to see it the first Sunday it was shown. He almost didn't recognize the place. There had been two owners since his parents had sold it 25 years earlier. Each had remodeled it. Walls were missing, the patio was now a deck and the landscaping was completely new. Seeing his old house look so different was unsettling to Bob. It made him want to buy it, and restore it, all the more.

The owner was asking six times what his parents had spent when they built the place 50 years earlier. Bob expected as much, and he knew restoring it would be expensive, maybe even doubling the asking price.

But he went for it, and his offer was accepted within hours. Bob was ecstatic.

He gave his wife the good news. She seemed indifferent. He expected her to be more excited, if not for herself, then for Bob.

He emailed his siblings. They were all surprised. One of his brothers thought Bob was kidding. All of them said congratulations but not much more.

Bob knew his parents would be happy, if they were still alive.

A few weeks later, Bob closed on the house. In the meantime, he began working with a contractor on a plan to remodel the whole place.

His goal was to make it look and feel just like it did when he was a kid. They worked from Bob's memory and old photographs. By the closing, the remodeling plan was complete, with a price tag twice as large as Bob had estimated. His wife wasn't happy, but she grudgingly agreed on the condition they take two family vacations the following year.

There were moments when Bob himself had doubts about buying the old place. But once the work began, and old, familiar walls, rooms and cabinets reemerged, Bob felt like a kid again, and he knew he'd made the right choice.

Once the reconstruction was complete, Bob hired an interior designer to decorate the place just as it was when he was growing up, from the red sofa to the black rotary telephones. He hired a landscape designer to replicate the outside too.

It was pricey. By the time the makeover was complete, Bob's investment was nearly three times what he'd expected. But he didn't mind, although his wife insisted on a third vacation the following year.

To Bob, it was well worth it. The place now looked spectacular, virtually identical to his childhood home. Inspecting it inside and out, Bob felt as though he had been transported back in time, and what a blissful time it was.

He couldn't wait to share it with his brothers and sisters. He decided to invite them all to spend the weekend there.

But they all declined. Everyone claimed they were busy, but in truth, they simply weren't interested.

So Bob invited his own children to spend the weekend. After all, for them, it was grandma and grandpa's house. They had loved the place as kids. But their lives were busy now, including with their own children. They all declined too.

"Well, I guess it's just going to be us," Bob said to his wife.

"Well, you're half right," she said. "Enjoy yourself."

Bob was disappointed that he wouldn't have any company, but he was still excited about the prospect of staying in his old house, even if he was alone. He packed a bag, kissed his wife and took off.

He stowed his stuff in his old bedroom and went out to the family room to watch TV, an old black and white Zenith. The house had not been wired for cable, so there were only three channels, the major networks, just like in the old days. Bob quickly got bored with that programming, though, and turned the TV off. He'd almost forgotten how to do that without a remote.

Bob thought about going online, but there was no WiFi or internet connection.

He walked around the house, not sure of what to do. It was getting dark, so he decided to turn in early.

He changed into his pajamas and got into his old bed. Or he tried to anyway. It was way too small. He thought about sleeping in his parents' bed, but that just didn't seem right.

So he drew his knees up and tried to get comfortable. But he couldn't and ended up sleeping on the davenport.

He woke up in the middle of the night, wondering where he

was. This doesn't feel like home, he thought. And indeed it wasn't. He knew it hadn't been his home for a very long time.

Bob decided to put the house up for sale. It sold in less than a day. Financially, he took a big hit because he had to price it in line with the other older, no-frills houses in the neighborhood.

Bob learned you can't reclaim your youth, no matter how hard you try or how much you spend. It was an expensive lesson.

The following year, he and his wife took four vacations, one of them in the south of France. It was there that Bob decided to try his hand at painting.

Flashpoint

Pete and I had been kayaking for about an hour in Glacier Bay, Alaska, when we spotted something in the distance. It looked like a shadow on the water. At first, I thought it was a boat. But then it disappeared — then reappeared. It was probably 200 yards away. Whatever it was, it was big.

"Holy crap!" Pete cried. "I think it's a whale!"

I felt my chest tighten. I felt dizzy. I had just learned to control my lifelong fear of water, and now it came rushing back. I had an overwhelming urge to get the hell out of this little boat and feel the earth beneath my feet.

I looked around to find our group. Once again, Pete and I had wandered off. We were 100 yards from the others. And we were all a mile from the small ship that all 14 of us called home that week.

"Pete, let's get back with the group," I said.

"No way," he said. "We're staying put. John said if we see a whale, we shouldn't move."

"Maybe it's not a whale."

"You're right!" Pete shouted. "It's not a whale. It's three whales!"

Sure enough, I now saw three whales in the distance, and they were heading our way.

Damn! Sometimes I hated it when Pete was right.

A week before, Pete and I had put our laptops away, kissed our families goodbye and set out for Alaska. It was July 2007.

I had known Pete for nearly 20 years. For much of that time, he had been asking me to take this trip with him. Pete had been to Alaska twice. He raved about it. His voice would get high-pitched, like a kid, when he told me about glaciers "calving icebergs," huge chunks of ice breaking off the end of glaciers and plummeting into the bay.

"They're as big as a school bus!" he would exclaim, stretching out his arms and thrusting his fingers into the air. "You're kayaking along and, all of a sudden, crack! The next thing you know, that ice hits the water, and the impact creates a huge wave. If you're too close, it'll swamp you and flip your boat. But if you're just far enough away, you can ride it. What a rush!"

Breathlessly, Pete told me about the time he dove off the side of a boat, without a wetsuit, into the frigid water below.

"It was a sunny day, but the water was 38 degrees," he said. "There was ice floating in it. Without a wetsuit, you've only got a few minutes to live. After a minute, your arms begin to freeze. So you can't jump out too far, and you have to swim fast."

Pete said when he hit the water, it was like being in another world.

"Everything is deep blue," he said. "You can't believe how cold that water is. At first, it stings like hell. Then you can't feel a thing. And you can't hear anything, except for the beating of your heart.

Boomp, boomp. Boomp, boomp. Boomp, boomp," Pete murmured, thumping his chest.

Yet Pete kept diving. He forced himself to go deeper until he could go no farther. When he finally surfaced, he heard the cheers of the other passengers watching from the safety of the deck.

"I was out farther than I thought," he said.

When he realized just how far from the boat he was, Pete tried to swim hard. He was a strong swimmer. But now his arms felt like lead, and he struggled to lift them. Tiny icebergs bounced off his 250-pound body. He felt like he was in slow motion. By the time he got close to the boat, he could barely move, and he could no longer feel his arms.

"But our guide was watching everything," he said, smiling, "and he pulled me up on deck just in time. It was incredible!"

Of course, none of us believed him. Who would do something so crazy?

But Pete had proof: a photograph someone on the boat had taken of him in the water. He carried it, folded and tattered, in his wallet. Sure enough, there was Pete--a walrus of a man, mustache and all, his blanched, bare torso jutting out of the icy water, his right arm extended forward and up, his hand grasping another man's hand, his lips blue, his thinning hair glazed on his forehead, his eyes half-closed. He was probably seconds from hypothermia. But on his face was a big grin that said: I made it — and I can't wait to tell you about it.

For years, Pete had tried to persuade me to go with him to Alaska. I was tempted. It certainly looked stunning in his pictures. But his stories--about glaciers calving, water so cold it could kill you, being chased in his kayak by a sea lion, hikers falling into deep crevasses--also scared the hell out of me.

Pete was a risk taker. In the 1980s, he had founded an advertising agency in Cincinnati, our hometown. Early on, he nearly lost everything. Once he had to mortgage his house to pay his employees. He always put others first. I admired that.

But Pete stuck with it--and it worked. He built his company into Cincinnati's largest ad agency. It became the place to work, especially if you were young in the business. It wasn't just successful. It was hip. Employees brainstormed while shooting pool in a conference room, Pete right along with them. He might have been old enough to be their father. But the other dads didn't sport a goatee, dress in black, tweet and bring home from Cannes a Gold Lion, one of the advertising industry's most prestigious awards.

And Pete's years of hard work paid off. In 2005, he sold his company to the biggest ad agency in the world for a small fortune. Pete's risk was also his reward.

I, on the other hand, was not a risk taker. I worked in public relations for one of the most conservative companies in the world. In 2007, I had been there for 27 years.

And while Pete was diving into ice water and being chased by sea lions, I was busy defending the safety of the latest controversial ingredient in shampoo.

But as different as our lives were, as different as we were, Pete and I became the best of friends. Part of it, I think, is that we balanced each other out.

But there was something more. I think Pete and I also became good friends because we could just be ourselves with each other.

At work, and even at home, we had roles to play, important roles, roles we loved. But the more we got into these roles, the harder it was to get out of them, to find an escape hatch, a way to step out and let down, to talk freely, to share problems without feeling obliged to also propose solutions.

This was the safe haven that Pete and I found, a place where we could be unguarded and unvarnished, a place void of pretense, a place of vulnerability, a place of pure acceptance.

We met through our wives, who met through our children. But I don't remember ever meeting Pete. Suddenly, he was just there, and we were hanging out, running together, drinking wine and telling jokes. We went to movies, dinner and baseball and football games together. We played golf, badly, together. We argued a lot, especially over politics and religion. We talked or texted nearly every day. And at some point, without ever saying so, we became best friends.

Pete kept asking me to go to Alaska, and I kept saying no. We would have to go in July, he said, the only time it was warm enough. And every July, I'd have a good excuse.

But the truth is: I was wary. For starters, I'm a poor swimmer, and I'm uncomfortable in the water. I wasn't sure I could handle being on a little boat and paddling around in a sea kayak in ice water for a week.

But Pete never gave up. And finally, in 2007, I said yes. Even now, I'm not really sure why I gave in. Maybe Pete just wore me down. Or maybe, after decades of trying to control things, I decided it was time to let go.

Pete was thrilled and went into fast motion. Within 24 hours, he had booked everything--the boat, flights, ground transportation and a place where we'd spend our first night in a tiny town called Gustavus, about 40 miles from Juneau, on the Gulf of Alaska.

We met in the Seattle airport on a Saturday afternoon. Pete had flown in from Cincinnati. I had flown in from Myrtle Beach, where I had just spent a week on a family vacation. When I got there, I saw that Pete had sent a text message to tell me he was in the Seattle Tap Room in Concourse B.

Pete was a man of extremes. At times, he could drink a lot and drink fast. All told, we had a brief, seven-beer layover.

From Seattle, we flew to Juneau, another two and half hours north. The airport there is the size of a convenience store. We boarded an eight-passenger Cessna for the 20-minute flight to Gustavus.

We flew low the whole time. Just below, I saw rivers, lakes, lagoons, mountains and glaciers.

As we were about to land, I could finally see the bay. It was dark blue and narrower than I had expected. I'd seen rivers as wide. But it seemed to extend forever, separating and branching out through the snow-capped mountains, more like a web of rivers than a bay.

But what really grabbed my attention were the glaciers. For some reason, I had always had trouble wrapping my mind around the idea of glaciers. As a city boy, I used to confuse them with icebergs.

Pete set me straight. He explained that icebergs are chunks of ice that break off from glaciers. Many are big--like the one the Titanic hit. Some are tiny, the size of ice cubes. All glaciers, though, are huge. Some stretch for hundreds of miles. They move slowly through the mountains and valleys, scouring the earth, always advancing and retreating.

Still, I had a hard time envisioning them. But then, from the plane, I saw them. They looked nothing like icebergs. They were a confluence of white, blue and grey. They looked like great tentacles, snaking through the mountain ranges like giant, frozen rivers. Some of them stretched beyond my field of vision, even at 5000 feet.

"There it is!" Pete exclaimed from his seat in front of me, pointing down at the bay. "Isn't it incredible?"

Good Lord, it was breathtaking — the most majestic landscape I'd ever seen. But it looked wild and daunting too, and I wondered what I had gotten myself into.

. . .

We landed on a runway that seemed far too short, descended the shaky aluminum stairs to the tarmac and grabbed our duffel bags from the belly of the plane. We slung them over our shoulders and lugged them through the tiny airport to the parking lot.

From there, a van took us to the inn, 10 minutes away. As soon as we left, I knew I was in a very special place.

The land was flat and rolled out in grassy prairies in every direction, surrounded by tall, dark evergreens rimmed by low, blue-green, snow-capped mountains in the distance. We passed a dozen houses, a few lodges, a school, a small general store, a library, two restaurants and a gas station with old-time, red pumps. The whole scene reminded me of one of those 1930s westerns that's been colorized.

Then suddenly we pulled into the long driveway of an inn.

It was large and white, two-storied, with a reddish-brown roof. I could tell from all the angles and windows that there were many rooms inside. The front lawn was 50 yards wide, and the grass smelled freshly cut. On one side stood a wall of towering, dark green fir trees. On the other, a rolling meadow of tall grasses and wildflowers.

Just beyond the meadow, extending behind the building, was a sprawling garden, with alternating rows of vegetables and flowers-- pansies, fuchsia, petunias, carnations, marigolds, snapdragons, sweet-peas, poppies, lupines and geraniums — in waves of red, white, pink, lavender, blue, orange and yellow. I was surprised to see such a vibrant display of flowers in a climate so harsh.

A split-rail fence framed the back and one side of the garden, some of it covered by blackberry, raspberry and red currant bushes. The air smelled earthy and sweet, a blend of rhubarb, flowers and pines. Beyond the garden stood an orchard, whose trees marched single file into the woods at the base of a broad, low mountain, the backdrop to everything. It was a scene that was at once wild and tamed, natural and crafted.

The owners of the inn were gracious hosts. We ate very well that evening. After dinner, we sampled the local craft beers at a small bar next to the kitchen.

Even though it wasn't dark yet — in July, the sun doesn't set in Alaska until about 10:00 — we were exhausted. So we headed to our rooms. I closed the curtains to block the early sunrise, then slipped into bed.

My alarm went off at 7:00, but the hearty scents of bacon, eggs and coffee had already roused me.

I had slept like a man who had traveled 3000 miles on a beer-of-the-month-club trip the day before. Still, I was tempted to snooze a little longer. But then, someone started banging on my door.

"Time for breakfast!" Pete shouted. I just knew his goofy face was scrunched up against my door.

"Get up, Don! We've got to be at the dock in an hour."

I was just stirring some blueberries into my oatmeal when folks began to get up, go to their rooms and check out. Soon, I was the only one left at the table — which was fine by me, since I was packed and ready to go.

I savored my oatmeal, buttered some toast, sipped my coffee and sat alone, facing two large windows along the back wall of the inn. The glass was thick — to withstand the harsh winters, I guessed. The garden flowers were brilliant in the morning sun, and they swayed in the breeze. And through the glass, awash with light, all the colors of the garden danced and blended together, like a kaleidoscope.

And I remembered it was Sunday. It felt like a Sunday morning in church. I knew it was cool outside. But with the sunlight streaming in, the air in the dining room was warm, and I felt radiant and so grateful for everything, including for Pete, for his persistence, for being there and for the courage to have finally said yes.

We boarded our small ship at a place called Bartlett Cove and set out for six days and six nights on Glacier Bay. There were nine passengers and five crew members. Our boat would cruise the bay by day and anchor in quiet coves at night. Most days, we went sea kayaking. Some days, we went hiking.

Now, on the first day, it was time to kayak. There were six kayaks in all: five two-man kayaks and a single for John, our guide.

"Let's go together, Don," Pete said. "You take the front, and I'll take the back."

I knew what that meant: Pete wanted to be in charge. I knew Pete was an experienced kayaker. He owned a kayak and took it out on a small lake near his house.

I didn't have nearly as much experience kayaking. But I had done a lot of canoeing as a kid. And I had done a couple of triathlons with Pete which included canoeing on the Little Miami River. I remembered he insisted on being in the back then too. We flipped our canoe about every mile.

"Are you sure?" I asked Pete.

"You worry too much," he replied. "Besides, we're wearing wetsuits."

Pete could be so confidence-inspiring.

"Hey, guys!" John yelled. "Don't go very far."

I'm glad he did because Pete had already started paddling away.

"Pete," I said. "John said to stay close."

"Don't worry," he replied. "I'm just getting us into position."

Pete liked to say that kind of crap, knowing it made absolutely no sense. I knew him, though. He just wanted to see how far he could go before John called us back.

"Hey, guys!" John yelled, as if on cue.

Pete stopped paddling. We glided to a stop.

I looked around. What had seemed big from the air, as we flew in yesterday, was now nearly too massive to comprehend.

Our boat had anchored in the middle of a narrow stretch of the bay. In front of me rose a glacier, stormy blue and powder white. It must have been 150 feet tall.

On the other side of the bay, behind us, stood a temperate rain forest. The tall evergreens were covered with mosses and lichens. I could see wildflowers and the trunks of downed trees along the forest floor. Streams flowed like fingers out of the woods, trickling down the rocky shore through brown moss-covered boulders and into the bay.

And surrounding everything were mountains that rose thousands of feet and stretched farther than I could see. The bay itself seemed endless too, like the ocean.

And there we were, Pete and I, in the center of all this, sitting in a 16-foot plastic kayak, floating, like a leaf on a pond, best friends, saying nothing, directing nothing, wanting nothing, just floating, immersed in a new world, a larger world, for a moment, this moment, together.

All six kayaks were now in the water. John reminded us to stick together. Then he pulled a large, expensive-looking Nikon camera from his kayak. He told us that in addition to being a tour guide, he was a professional photographer. He said he would be taking our pictures all week.

And with that, as a group, we headed toward an enormous glacier. The closer we got, the more ice I saw in the water. At first, it was in the form of tiny icebergs, no bigger than ice cubes.

"Grab one, Don," Pete said, leaning over and scooping one up in his hand. "Taste it," he said, popping it in his mouth and chomping on it like candy. "This is the oldest ice cube you'll ever have."

I reached out and snagged one. The water was freezing. The ice cube was clear and slick, and I could see small stone particles and air bubbles inside. I licked it and put it in my mouth. But with all that debris inside, I decided against biting it. It tasted clean. I guess I was expecting it to taste like salt — or dirt. I sucked on it for a minute, numbing my tongue. Then I spit it back into the sea.

We kept paddling toward the glacier. The icebergs were getting larger, some now the size of basketballs, others as big as cars. Some were square, some flat, some domed. Pete maneuvered us through them, the smallest ones bouncing off the sides of our kayak. Then, a few hundred yards from the glacier, John yelled: "Stop everybody!"

We all stopped paddling.

"Quiet," he said. "Listen. Just listen."

At first, I wasn't sure what he meant. Then I heard something popping, crackling, the sound echoing off the glacier.

"This glacier is melting," John told us. "Every glacier melts. But now they're melting faster than ever. That popping is the sound of air bubbles escaping from the ice. The ice is constantly melting, so that popping sound never stops."

Suddenly, we heard a much louder noise — like a clap of thunder. A huge chunk of ice had broken off the middle of the glacier in front of us. It slid down the face, leaving a cascade of snow and ice in its trail. The ice exploded into the water, creating a broad wave, which rolled toward us, slowly.

I looked around for John. He shouted not to worry, it wasn't a "big one." He said to just point our kayaks toward the wave and ride it. Pete re-oriented us, and I had to back paddle hard to give us enough time to square up. The first wave was now just seconds away.

"Hold on, Don," Pete said. "Here it comes!"

I watched as the wave hit us straight on, then felt it go under our boat, rocking us, front to back. It was like riding a kids' roller-coaster — except surrounded by about a million gallons of ice water. I pushed my paddle down hard against the top of our kayak to steady myself.

"Holy shit!" Pete shouted. "What a rush!"

"Thank God," I sighed, relieved we were still upright.

"I can't believe we saw calving on the first day," Pete said. "This is going to be a great trip!"

Everyone was hooting and hollering — and Pete and I hadn't flipped our boat. Maybe he knew what he was doing after all.

After checking out the glacier a bit more, but still at a safe distance, we all turned around and headed for the other shore. It was as lush as the other was frozen. On this side was an old-growth forest of massive hemlock and spruce trees. They stretched up and down the shore line as far as I could see — a rocky, jagged shore line, etched with inlets and coves.

For the next hour or so, we would explore several of those coves. Along the way, we began to see an astonishing array of wildlife. We saw sea otters with brown fur, the size of puppies, floating on their backs, looking surprisingly carefree. We saw several bald eagles. Until then, I'd never seen even one. We saw dozens of puffins, which John described perfectly as "flying potatoes." And near the shore, we looked down into the clear water and saw large red, blue, green, yellow, even purple, starfish.

Pete and I began to drift away from the others, toward the center of the bay. We hadn't strayed far, but far enough to make me a little uneasy.

"Pete, let's stay with the group," I said.

"I'm keeping them in sight," Pete said. "We're fine. You worry too much."

Maybe he was right. Maybe I was worrying too much. Pete had been here twice before. He did seem to know what he was doing, and he hadn't steered me wrong so far. I guess I just needed to learn to relax.

Then suddenly, Pete cried: "Look! I think it's a sea lion!"

Oh God, I thought. I turned around to see Pete. He was pointing ahead to our left. I pivoted back around and looked out — and saw something big thrashing near the middle of the bay. It was less than 100 feet away.

"Let's go take a look," Pete said. I felt our kayak surge forward.

"Come on, Pete," I said. "Those things are dangerous."

"It's not going to bother us," he replied. "It's busy. It's eating lunch."

As we got closer, I realized it was indeed a sea lion. It was huge — I guessed maybe 10 feet long and 1000 pounds. It was dark brown, with black fins, a small head, thick neck, flat nose, long whiskers and bulging black eyes.

I stopped paddling, but Pete didn't, and so we inched closer to the beast. I could see its mouth now — and its teeth: four long, curved canines in the front with rows of cone-shaped incisors behind. When I saw those teeth, "sea lion" suddenly made sense.

And it was indeed eating lunch. It had caught a king salmon. It probably weighed 30 pounds, but the sea lion tossed it high in the air, like a rag doll, tearing it apart. Blood and pieces of flesh and bone flew everywhere. And with each toss, the sea lion would take another bite of the fish, its head snapping back, like a ravenous dog chomping on a piece of raw meat.

"Pete, stop," I said in a loud whisper.

Now we were only about 20 feet away — close enough, apparently, even for Pete because he finally stopped paddling. We glided to a stop and just sat there, transfixed as the predator violently, powerfully devoured the last of its poor prey.

Then the beast looked at us, opened its mouth wide, made a deep, growling, menacing sound and slipped under the surface of the water.

"Hey, guys!" John yelled, breaking our trance. "Get back here!"

I turned around to see him. He and the other kayakers were 100 yards behind us.

Then I caught a glimpse of Pete. He was just sitting there, his paddle resting in front of him, with a big smile on his face. He was quiet. Pete was seldom quiet. I think he was happy. I think he was happy that we had just witnessed something so wild and intense and that we hadn't kept our distance. I think he was happy that we had seen that glacier calve and ridden the wave. I think he was happy to have steered us through those icebergs. I think he was happy to be back in Alaska and showing me the ropes. And although he never said so, in that moment, I think Pete was very happy to be alive.

And I was happy too. I was happy to be guided for a change, to let go, to give up control. I was happy to leave my familiar world behind and enter this mysterious new one. I was happy to unplug. I was happy that this adventure was just beginning. I was happy at the prospect of not shaving for a week. And, of course, I was happy that I hadn't just been eaten by a sea lion.

· · ·

The next morning, we all shuffled into the galley for breakfast. John was sitting at the end of the table, drinking coffee and bidding us good morning.

As we munched on bagels, he told us that this morning we would kayak to Margerie Glacier. There, we would paddle to shore near the edge of the glacier and eat lunch. Then we would hike up the side of a mountain which borders the glacier.

"If everybody's up for it, we should be able to climb up about 2000 feet and see about 10 miles of the bay," Dave said. "The view is spectacular!"

Two hours later, we were climbing that mountain. The trail was steep, narrow and very rocky. The brush — tall grasses and bushes — was coarse and thick. The climb was a struggle, and we had to stop several times to rest. But at about 2000 feet, we reached a plateau. There, we all stopped and looked out over the bay.

John was right: we could see for miles. In the bright sun, the bay looked like a giant mirror. Everything was reflected in it — mountains, forests, glaciers, even the sky. Everything was revealed in the water.

The air was cool, and the wind bore the scent of everything below us: the trees, the rocks, the moss, the salt water, the ice. The fragrance of all these things rose up to meet us on the wind, and I closed my eyes and breathed it in.

And for a moment, I did not feel separate from these things. I felt one with them and everything. And I felt I had known this once, long ago — and that if I could be still and open, as I was at that moment, I could know it again.

That night, Pete and I lay awake for a while in our bunks. I told him about my experience on the mountain that day, about my feeling of communion with everything.

I thought he might laugh or start snoring. But he listened and said he had had a similar feeling himself — the last time he was in Alaska.

"I've never put it into words," he said. "But that's how I felt. I brought that feeling home with me, and I thought I'd never lose it. But I did. Now, though, I'm feeling it again. You're right. When you really think about it, it all begins to blend together."

Pete stopped talking, and I just listened. I thought maybe he had fallen asleep.

"Pete?"

"Yeah."

"Thanks."

"For what?"

"For bringing me here, for not giving up on me. For this whole thing."

"Sure," he said. "Good night, Don."

"Good night, Pete."

The next day, we "shot the arch," a massive arched iceberg carved by water, wind and time in a cove of the bay. The parabola-shaped opening was probably 50 feet tall but only about 20 feet wide. The water pulsed through it, tons of water, suddenly constrained and channeled, crashing violently against the walls of the arch in 10-foot surges. And when the water hit those walls, it sounded like thunder.

I could hardly imagine going through there in a kayak. But we all huddled around John in our kayaks near the entrance, and he told us how to do it. The trick, he said, is to stay in the middle, point your kayak toward the other end and just ride it.

"Don't try to steer or even paddle," he told us. "Just get out of the way and let it take you. Watch me."

Then, without hesitating, he showed us how by going first. Once we saw him ride the crest of those waves straight through, and come out alive, our spines stiffened — and everyone began lining up to go next.

Still, I knew this was not like any kayaking I had done in the past. And I now understood why John had made each of us bring a helmet that day. I fastened mine tight.

All week, Pete and I had kayaked together. Today, though, one of the crew members was my partner and another passenger was his. On one hand, I was sorry not to be doing this with Pete. But on the other, I got to watch him shoot the arch.

Pete and his new bowman were both big men. But going through the arch, with their helmets on, bobbing wildly, at the mercy of the waves, they looked like a couple of Fisher-Price little people in a toy boat.

Over the roar, I could hear their screams, echoing off the walls, screams of ecstasy, of pure joy, like children opening gifts on Christmas morning. Hearing that was as thrilling to me as my own turn through the arch.

And as I shot through, there was Pete waiting, cheering me on, looking as happy as I had ever seen him.

Friday would be our last day of sea kayaking.

We dropped anchor at a place in the bay called Adolphus Point. John told us it was a popular feeding spot for humpback whales. They spent their summers there, "rebuilding their blubber supply," he said, after migrating 3000 miles every year from Hawaii, where they mate and have babies.

We had hoped to see one, but at a distance--and from the ship! And yet here we were, Pete and I, watching breathlessly from our kayak as three humpbacks headed straight toward us.

Side by side, one by one, they dove under the surface of the water, then emerged, like giant pistons. As they did, they blew great puffs of misty spray into the air. Their exhaling made a gushing sound, like steam blasting from a locomotive. Their backs were mottled black. They were now less than 100 yards away.

John yelled to us to tap our paddles on our kayak. Of course! During our orientation the first day, he had told us to do this if we ever saw a whale, no matter how far away, so it would know where we were and not accidentally upend us.

I felt so small and vulnerable. My heart raced. I had no options. All I could do was wait, tap my paddle and hope the whales would hear us.

Then, suddenly, they were gone. Fifty feet away, the whales disappeared.

"Where did they go?" I asked.

"Oh, shit!" Pete said. "I think they're under the boat!"

"Keep tapping!" John shouted. Pete and I tapped our paddles furiously.

Then suddenly, a whale burst through the surface of the water ten feet in front of me. Boom! It must have been 50 feet long. I could have reached out and touched it with my paddle. Its skin was bumpy, like a cucumber. It had a small fin on its back. Barnacles encrusted the underside of its mouth. Its eye was the size of a baseball. It looked like a gigantic human eye--and it was staring right at me.

Whoosh, the whale blew its spray hard and high into the air.

The sound was so deep I could feel the vibration. Spray rained down on us. It tasted salty and fishy, like sardines.

Then a second whale burst through the surface, just to our left. Boom! Then a third, just to our right. Boom! They formed a crescent around us. And they were all blowing their spray into the air. We were soaked with it.

By now, it was clear the whales knew where we were, so Pete and I stopped tapping and just sat there and stared at them as they stared at us. They seemed content just to watch us and didn't come any closer. They hovered gracefully. I started breathing again.

And so there we were, the five of us, together, in a big ring in the sea. The whales began moaning, groaning, almost singing. It occurred to me that maybe they were communicating with each other. Or maybe with us.

A few moments ago, these enormous creatures had terrified me. But then, maybe out of desperation, I let go. And now, as I looked into their eyes, I was no longer afraid.

As Pete and I sat there, we did not speak. We had entered a wordless place, a place of stillness, a sacred place.

At some point, we realized that our friends were cheering. They had seen it all. And what Pete and I didn't know is that John had been taking pictures of us the whole time.

The next morning, after a late breakfast, our boat cruised into Bartlett Cove, where most of us had met just six days earlier. We were certainly not strangers now, though, and we didn't want to say goodbye.

A van was waiting at the dock to take us to the airport. But for a few minutes, we all lingered, hugging each other.

We promised to stay in touch. We said we'd see each other again. But we knew that wouldn't happen.

And it never did. Five years later, suddenly and unexpectedly, Pete died of a massive heart attack.

I've given up trying to make sense of Pete's death. But the more that time passes, and the more my specific memories of him fade and blur, the clearer I am on how our friendship changed me, how it opened and expanded me.

For me, our Alaska trip was the flashpoint.

There, I learned to let go, to let someone else steer. There, I remembered we are all connected and that I am not really separate from anything, not even the whales. There, I came to understand that that which had once seemed so foreign and even frightening to me had now become a part of me, just as it always had been.

I discovered these things in 2007 in Alaska with my friend Pete. He had waited for me a long time. He is waiting for me still.

But separation, I now know, is an illusion.

And so I close my eyes and see Pete, smiling in our kayak, chomping on a tiny iceberg, shooting the arch. I see him sitting in front of me on the plane, pointing down at Glacier Bay and saying, "Isn't it incredible?"

Karma

James was a good man, except on April Fool's Day. That was the day, when he was 28, his wife Linda left him. Every April Fool's Day since, James did things to get back at her.

"Karma's a bitch," he liked to say.

On that day, James did things he would never normally even consider. He damaged and destroyed property. He stole. He swore and said hurtful things.

Linda had wounded James deeply. The things he did on April Fool's Day made him feel he was giving back what was due. What goes around, comes around.

On the second of April, James didn't feel any better. But on the first, with his every bad deed, James told himself he was "making things right."

The years didn't slow him down or soften him. If anything, with each passing April Fool's Day, James became more destructive.

One year, on the last day of March, James set his plan for the following day. Shoplifting, "keying" cars in parking lots, spraying graffiti. He made a long list.

James had grown old. Just thinking about the day ahead made him tired, and he decided to go to bed early. He fell into a deep sleep. He dreamed he had died and was talking with God.

"Is this heaven?" James said.

"Not quite," said God.

"Well, am I going to heaven?"

"Not yet."

"Not yet? When?"

"When you've understood karma."

"But I do understand it!"

"You do?"

"Yeah, I practice it every April Fool's Day."

"That's not karma."

"It's not?"

"No," said God. "Karma doesn't take revenge."

"It doesn't?"

"No. Karma says the things you do in life will eventually return to you, in this life or the next."

James thought for a moment.

"*All* the things I do?" he said.

"Every one," said God.

"But Linda hurt me."

"Yes, she did, James, and now you have a choice. You can choose to act in a way that deepens that wound or heals it. But remember: whatever you choose will come back to you."

God vanished, and James slept on. When he finally woke up, his room was aglow in early-morning light. Thinking about what God had said in his dream, which seemed so very real, he decided to ditch his plan and spend the day doing good things.

James got up and went over to his desk. He sat down and pulled out a pen and a sheet of paper to make a list of ideas. But as he was about to jot them down, he instead wrote:

Dear Linda,

I'm sorry ...

Spiritual, Not Religious

Pete Loman watched blue-gray plumes of incense smoke rise like swirling spirits over the casket of his late wife as the priest swung a metal censer suspended from three gold chains. He remembered holding the censer open for his pastor when he was an altar boy so the priest could sprinkle powdery incense on charcoal discs which Pete had lit in the sacristy. It was a ritual Pete had nearly forgotten because he had not been to Mass or even inside a church for many years.

He had stopped going to church because of his wife, and now here she was, being blessed in the sanctuary of St. Augustine, a white pall draped over her casket, surrounded by dozens of family members and friends who had gathered to mourn her passing and pray for the repose of her soul.

Pete met Sarah Keller at a party at a mutual friend's house after work one Friday. Each caught the other's eye. They were both still dressed in business attire, he in a blue pinstriped suit befitting an investment banker, she in a black dress befitting a fashion designer. He had dark hair and an athletic build. She was blond and petite with a face as pretty as the models she dressed. His eyes were brown. Hers were blue. They both smiled easily.

They were happy to be seated across from one another for dinner. They discovered they had a lot in common. They were both from large families. They had both grown up in the Midwest and come to New York after taking master's degrees. They both lived alone in flats in Soho.

At first, Pete was struck by Sarah's beauty. Her skin glowed and her complexion was flawless, yet she wore little make-up. But the more they talked, the more he was drawn to her eyes. Not because they were lovely, although they were, but because of a certain sadness he detected there. It gave her depth and made Pete want to get to know her all the more.

As guests began to leave, Pete asked Sarah if he could call her sometime. She said yes, and they exchanged business cards. They shared an Uber back to Soho. She got dropped off first. As she got out, she reached over for his hand.

"I'll see you again," she said.

"Good night," Pete said, gently squeezing her small hand.

He woke up before dawn the next morning, thinking about her. He waited until 8:oo, then sent her a text.

I know it's a long shot, but by any chance would you be free for dinner tonight?

They met that evening at an Italian restaurant in an industrial-chic building in Soho. Pete took an Uber, but it was close enough to Sarah's place that she could walk.

Over dinner, they talked about everything from their childhoods to their jobs. As they talked, they held each other's gaze. To Pete, it was as if everyone else in the restaurant didn't exist. It was a noisy place, but he was completely focused on her voice, soft as it was.

And then there were her eyes. The more he looked into them, the deeper they seemed to go. It was as if he could see into her soul. What's more, he felt as though she were inviting him in, to see something more than her outward beauty, to behold something mysterious. In her eyes, he again sensed a sadness, just as he had the evening before. It drew him in, not as someone to light the darkness, but as a companion to hold her hand.

The restaurant began to clear out.

"It's getting late," Pete said. "You must be tired."

"Do you have an early morning?" she asked.

"Not too early. I was thinking of going to 9:00 Mass at St. Patrick's."

"Are you religious?" she asked.

"Sort of."

"Sort of?"

"Well, I go to church once in a while, if that's what you mean."

"I'd call that religious."

"Well, I used to be a lot more religious."

"You're Catholic?"

"Yeah," he said. "I was raised Catholic."

"I was too, but I haven't been to Mass since my high school graduation."

"Do you still consider yourself a Catholic?"

"No," she said.

"Why?" he asked, hoping he was not intruding.

"Well, I used to say I'm spiritual, not religious. But lately, I'm not so sure I'm all that spiritual either."

"Do you believe in God?"

"I don't know," she said. "I'm just not sure anymore."

He felt their conversation was getting a little too personal and thought it might be best to change the subject.

"May I walk you home?" he asked.

"I'd like that," she said.

They left the restaurant and stepped out onto the sidewalk. It was a warm night. As they turned and started walking, their hands touched. Pete reached for her hand, and she slipped it into his. She smiled and held his hand tightly, leaning into him, as they strolled down the sidewalk together.

When they got to her apartment, he pulled out his cell phone and said, "I'll call an Uber."

She turned to him and looked up into his face, her big, blue eyes gleaming in the lamplight like two oceans lit up by the moon. She stood on her toes and kissed him gently and slowly on the cheek.

"Why don't you come in?" she whispered.

He slipped his phone into his pocket, cupped her face in his hands and kissed her on the lips.

"Okay," he said between kisses.

Soon, Pete and Sarah fell in love. Six months later, they moved into an apartment in the tony Park Slope neighborhood in Brooklyn. Six months later, Pete proposed. A year after that, they were married at the charming Picnic House in Prospect Park.

Pete had suggested they get married in church.

"No way," Sarah said.

"Why not?" Pete asked.

"I'm just not comfortable there," she said. "Besides, we'd have to go through Pre-Cana. The priest would grill me about why I haven't been to church in 10 years. That wouldn't end well."

Pete didn't argue. He hadn't been to church lately himself.

And so they got married in an old building in a park in a ceremony that was decidedly secular. Their parents weren't thrilled about that, but Pete and Sarah paid for everything, so their parents didn't really get a vote.

Pete and Sarah were very happy together. They both worked long hours, but they made a point of having dinner together every night they were both home, no matter how late it was. On weekends, they toured museums, took in concerts and plays and went shopping. Sometimes Pete joined Sarah at fashion shows, including in Milan and Paris. They loved to travel.

They spent a small fortune on furnishings for their apartment. Sarah worked with an interior decorator on a complete makeover, which took more than a year. She was ecstatic when *House Beautiful* decided to include their place in a splashy feature on urban living. She bought reprints and sent them to colleagues and clients.

Sarah and Pete loved showing off their place. They hosted dinner parties every few months. Unfortunately, their dining room was relatively small, so they could invite only two other couples at a time.

They solved this problem by buying a brownstone just a few blocks away in Brooklyn. They got a good deal at just under $2 million. Their friends and relatives thought it was a sure sign Pete and Sarah were ready to start a family, but they saw it strictly as a smart investment—and, of course, a way to host larger dinner parties.

Before they got married, Pete and Sarah had discussed the idea of having children. Sarah was always cool to it. But now that they were well established in their careers and in their mid-thirties, Pete thought he would bring up the idea again. He asked Sarah over breakfast one Sunday.

Without answering him directly, she said, "When was the last time you saw Ben and Emily?"

"I don't know," he said. "It's been a while."

"Yeah, like about two years. Do you know why?"

"No, why?"

"Because they have kids now," she said. "Nobody ever sees them anymore."

"I think it would be fun to have kids," he said. "And I think you'd be a great mother."

"Please," she said. "I'd be the worst mother of all time. I have no patience for kids, and I've grown accustomed to our lifestyle, Pete. I like it. I'm afraid of what raising a family would do to my career. Imagine if we had to get by on one salary. I mean you're making great money, but we'd have to give a lot of things up. We might even have to sell this place. And imagine what college tuition is going to cost in 20 years."

Sarah's neck was red. Pete knew that meant she was truly upset. He decided not to push the subject, at least not at the moment. *Maybe she'll change her mind*, he thought. *We've still got plenty of time.*

Just after her thirty-sixth birthday, Sarah had her annual check-up with her gynecologist, Dr. Anna Costello. Sarah told her she had been experiencing some tenderness and slight pain in her left breast. She hadn't had a mammogram, so Dr. Costello ordered one just to be safe.

The next day, Dr. Costello called Sarah at work.

"It's probably nothing to be worried about, but we're seeing some spots in both your breasts."

"Spots?" Sarah said, trying not to sound alarmed.

"Yes, small, white spots. It's possible they've been there a while and are no real consequence. Since you haven't had a mammogram before, we have nothing to compare this one to."

"So what should we do?"

"Well, I'd like to get a better look," Dr. Costello said. "So I think we should do an MRI."

"Okay. When?"

"I can schedule you for as soon as tomorrow."

"Okay. Let's do it tomorrow."

"Good. I'll have someone call you right back to confirm the time."

"Anna," Sarah said. "Do you think it's cancer?"

"I don't know. What I do know is that mammograms can sometimes give false positives for cancer, especially in younger patients, like you. So I don't think we should jump to any conclusions. I wish I could be more specific. We'll know a lot more after tomorrow."

The MRI showed stage 3 cancer in both breasts. Sarah and Pete met right away with an oncologist, Dr. Whitacre. His recommended treatment was chemotherapy, which Sarah received in a clinic over the course of 12 weeks. After that, she had another MRI to assess the results.

Unfortunately, the tumors were not "meaningfully changed," and Dr. Whitacre recommended a radical mastectomy, concluding more limited surgery would likely not be successful.

Six weeks after her surgery, Sarah saw Dr. Whitacre for a follow-up exam. Her blood results showed the presence of cancer. A full-body MRI showed tumors in her liver and lungs.

"What are our treatment options?" Pete asked, sitting next to Sarah.

"I think chemotherapy is our best course," Dr. Whitacre said. "It gives us the best way of killing cancer cells wherever they may be in Sarah's body."

"What are my chances of survival?" Sarah asked.

"If the chemotherapy is effective, 30%," he said.

"And if I don't do chemo again?" Sarah asked.

"You wouldn't make it, Sarah," he said.

"Let's do it then," she said, squeezing Pete's hand.

This time, Sarah's chemotherapy was administered in the hospital, four days at a time. There would be six treatments in all, with a week off in between. The whole thing would take three months.

Sarah had tolerated the first chemotherapy regimen fairly well and, for the most part, she was able to keep working. This new regimen, though, consisting of a new cocktail of toxic drugs, hit her very hard. She threw up every day, slept a lot and began losing weight rapidly. She had no choice but to stop working.

When Sarah was in the hospital, Pete visited her there every day. When he could, he worked from her hospital room. When he talked on the phone, he sometimes disturbed Sarah, so he began using any empty room he could find when he needed to make a call. It was hardly ideal, but he would rather be near her than not.

As the treatment wore on and Sarah grew weaker, Pete asked her if she would like to see a priest.

"No priest," she said.

He didn't bring it up again.

By the fifth week of treatment, Sarah was pale, weak and emaciated. One morning, Pete arrived with the breakfast she had ordered the night before: a fried egg on buttered wheat toast. Her sense of taste changed all the time, and she hated hospital food.

He was putting her food on a plate when she said, "Would you hold onto that, please? I think I need to sleep a little longer."

"Of course," he said, leaning down and kissing her bald head.

"Thank you," she said, drifting off to sleep.

Pete went down the hall and put Sarah's breakfast in a refrigerator in the nurses' lounge. He had grown used to storing food and drinks there.

When he got back to her room, Sarah was asleep. He looked down at her. She had a most peaceful look on her face. He sat down in a recliner and pulled out his laptop to get some work done.

A few minutes later, he heard Sarah say, "Wow."

He looked over at her. She was looking up at the ceiling.

"Are you okay?" Pete asked.

She lowered her gaze and turned her head toward him. He looked at her face. It was luminous. Then he looked into her eyes. They were bright and, for the first time in a very long time, there was no trace of sadness.

"Yeah," she said. "Was it real?"

"Was what real?"

"What I just saw," she said.

"I don't know. What did you see?"

"I saw God."

"God?"

"Yeah."

"What did he look like?"

"It's hard to say. He isn't—he isn't any one thing."

Pete sat there, not sure what to say.

"He is everything," she said. "And everywhere."

She closed her eyes.

"I need to sleep some more," she said.

"Okay," he said. "I'll be right here."

She fell back to sleep, a most peaceful look once again on her face. This time, she slept for an hour.

Pete was just about to step out to make a call when he heard her say softly, "Good morning."

"Good morning," he said. "How are you feeling?"

"I feel nothing," she said.

"Let me call the nurse," he said.

"No, Pete," she said. "I'm okay. Just sit. I have something to tell you."

He got out of the recliner, pulled a wooden chair up to her bed and sat down beside her. He took her left hand in both of his hands.

"What is it?" he asked.

"I was wrong," she said. "There is a God, and I *am* spiritual."

Pete gently squeezed her hand.

"I'm still not religious," she said, with a little laugh. "But I am spiritual. We all are."

"We are? How do you know?"

"Because I've seen God. I saw him in the faces of children. He is here. He is alive in us."

"I believe you," Pete said, tears rolling down his cheeks.

"Pete, you have to do something for me," she said.

"What it is, Sarah?"

"You have to take everything I own and sell it and give the money to the poor."

"Everything?"

"Yes, everything."

"Why?"

"I told you once I didn't believe in God," she said. "But the truth is, I've made the things I own into a god, and I've been selfish. I want to give away everything I have. Will you do that for me?"

"Yes," he said. "I will."

"Thank you, Pete. You're a good man."

He gently squeezed her hand.

"I'm going back to sleep now," she said. "Good night."

"Good night, my love," he said, getting up, leaning over and kissing her on the cheek.

He went back to the recliner and sat down. He had never felt so tired. He lay back and fell into a deep sleep.

A little while later, he was awakened by a loud, shrill beep and the sound of an anxious voice.

"She's not breathing!" Sarah's nurse called into a speaker in the wall.

One evening, a few weeks after Sarah's funeral, Pete sat on the sofa in his living room, looking at a picture of the two of them, taken in Paris a few years earlier. They both looked so happy, and she looked so elegant. They had just finished watching a fashion show and, in her little black dress, Sarah looked like she could have been on the runway.

He was still grieving her loss, but knowing he had still not acted on her dying wish made his heart even heavier. But he wasn't sure how to go about giving away Sarah's wealth. After all, she had not been specific, and there was nothing in their will about it.

He thought back to his childhood, when he used to pray for enlightenment when he was uncertain about things. He used to pray in church. But then he went to Mass nearly every day. He hadn't been in a church since the funeral at St. Augustine's. It was the only time he'd been there. *Maybe I should go back.*

He went online to see when St. Augustine's offered Mass. During the week, there was a Mass every morning at 7:00. He decided he would go in the morning and ask God for guidance.

The church was just a few blocks away from his home, so Pete walked there the next morning. He got there about 6:45. There were two large, wooden doors at the entrance. An old man with long gray hair and a long beard in loose-fitting, tattered clothes was sitting on the doorstep, right between the two doors. There was a basket on the sidewalk in front of him.

Pete wasn't sure if he could step around the man in order to open one of the doors.

"Excuse me," he said.

"Going to church?" the beggar asked.

"Yes," Pete said.

"Doors don't open until just before seven."

Pete looked at his watch.

"You can wait here," said the beggar.

"I guess I will," Pete said.

He looked down into the basket. It was empty. He took out his wallet. The smallest bill he had was a five. He pulled it out and dropped it into the basket.

"Thank you," the beggar said.

"You're welcome."

A small boy, wearing a book bag on his back, was walking by them down the sidewalk.

"Good morning, King," the beggar said to him.

"Good morning, Mr. Ackmann," the boy said.

"Had breakfast?" the beggar asked.

"No," the boy replied.

"Got money for lunch?"

"No."

"Here," the beggar said, pulling the five out of his basket and handing it to the boy.

"Thank you!" said the boy.

"You're welcome, King. God be with you today."

Pete heard someone unlocking the doors from the inside.

"Are you coming in?" he asked the beggar.

"No," he said. "My church is out here."

Pete reached for the wrought iron door handle, then stopped. In his mind, he heard Sarah's voice.

I saw him in the faces of children.

He took out his wallet, pulled out all the money inside, and placed it in the beggar's basket.

"Thank you," said Mr. Ackmann. "That's going to make a lot of kids happy.

The Door

As I lay dying, I awoke. My room was filled with soft white light. In the near distance, I saw a door.

I went over, opened it and stepped through. Looking around, I realized I was standing before my childhood home. Everything was just as it was then, even me.

I looked back at the open door. I sensed I could close it and stay there and live my life over again. Maybe then I could make better choices.

But I knew my choices were a part of me, and I turned around and stepped back through the door.

The Olive Tree

Arjun Agarwal and Akeyo Kamau met during their first year of medical school at Johns Hopkins. Arjun was from India, Akeyo from Kenya. Both were new to the US.

They had seen each other in biochemistry. Each was instantly attracted to the other. He moved closer to her in class, sitting just behind her in order to watch her discretely. But she knew he was there and suspected his eyes were upon her.

One day, as class was letting out, he approached her.

"Hello," he said, looking nervous.

"Hello," she said, feigning surprise.

"My name is Arjun," he said, extending his hand.

"I am Akeyo," she said, taking it.

After making small talk about the class, he said, "I hope you will not think me too forward, but would you like to get coffee sometime?"

"Well, that is a bit forward," she said.

"I'm sorry —,"

"I'd love to," she said with a smile.

Arjun and Akeyo began falling in love over their first coffee together. Her light brown skin and dark eyes drew him in. His strong, stubbled jawline quickened the pace of her breath.

He asked her to dinner, and she said yes. He took her to a restaurant which advertised East African fare. The meat, vegetables and rice dishes were weak imitations of the foods she had known, but they made her feel a bit more at home, and she was grateful for his thoughtfulness.

During their third year of medical school, Arjun proposed to Akeyo. They were married in Baltimore right after their graduation and just before they both started their residencies in dermatology. Five years later, when they were both in private practice, their daughter was born.

They named her Olivia not just because her skin was olive but because Olivia, in both Indian and Kenyan, means olive tree, a tree they had both known growing up.

Olivia was the only child Arjun and Akeyo would choose to have. They spoiled her, giving her all the things they had missed as children. Most of all, they wanted Olivia to have a first-class education. For Arjun and Akeyo, education had been their path out of poverty and to a brighter and more prosperous future than anyone else in their families had ever known.

They dreamed their daughter would, just like her parents, become a doctor one day. And so even as early as kindergarten, they encouraged Olivia to focus on science and math.

But Olivia had no interest in these subjects. The only things that seemed to interest her in school were reading and art. When Arjun and Akeyo learned this, they were horrified. They considered reading and art soft pursuits and of no value to Olivia, especially if she were to become a doctor.

And so they discouraged her from spending time on such useless subjects, and they spent even more time helping her with science and math.

Olivia's heart wasn't in such things, but she was a dutiful daughter, and she tried to heed her parents' advice. But she had little aptitude for science and math. The best grade she could ever earn in these subjects, even with a tutor, was a B. Arjun and Akeyo worried this would bring down her GPA and hurt her chances of eventually getting into medical school. Fortunately, the As she earned in English, art and history brought up her GPA. Olivia loved these subjects, even though her parents called them "a waste of time."

In school, Olivia was unique. There were lots of Black and Indian kids, but no one else was of a blend of the two. Olivia looked like no one else. What's more, she was striking with thick, black hair, almond-shaped brown eyes, light brown skin and full, red lips. Her beauty made her unpopular with many of the girls, who were jealous, and appealing to most of the boys. In high school, boys were constantly asking her out.

"What do they see in me?" she asked a friend.

"Don't be naive," her friend said. "You're gorgeous, and no one else looks like you. You're mysterious. Guys love that."

"But they don't even know me."

"Oh, come on. That doesn't matter. Guys know what they want based on what they see. That's all they need to know."

This made Olivia sad. How could people be so superficial? How could none of the guys who asked her out ever once ask about her interests?

Adding to her funk, Olivia's parents had begun insisting that she apply to Johns Hopkins and major in pre-med.

"But I don't want to be a doctor," she told her mother.

"That's what you think now," Akeyo said. "Wait until your

junior year. By then, you can decide, and you will have fulfilled all your science and math requirements, regardless of which path you choose."

"Thanks, Mom," Olivia said, dreading the idea of pre-med but, for the first time, feeling hopeful that her parents might eventually allow her to pursue her true interests.

Olivia hated biology, chemistry and calculus at Johns Hopkins. At the end of her first semester, she had a C in all three classes. But she loved English comp and world history, getting an A in each of them.

Though her GPA was 3.2, her parents were concerned about her low grades in science and math.

"You'll never get into med school with those grades," her father said.

"I'm not going to med school, Dad," she said.

"Well, then, maybe I'll stop paying for your education," Arjun said.

"Now, Arjun," Akeyo said. "I told Olivia she could decide whether she'll continue with pre-med when she's a junior. But I know she won't disappoint us and switch majors then."

It was closest her mother had ever come to supporting her right to choose her own way, but it ended with a threat. Sometimes Olivia wondered if she was her parents' daughter or their project.

The second semester of her freshman year was even heavier on science, with labs as well as lectures in both biology and chemistry. This left Olivia the option of one elective. She chose an art class.

The teacher was a small, goateed man named Mr. Nagy. What a shame, Olivia thought, that the art instructors here don't merit being called professor.

The class met in the school's art studio. During the first class, Nagy explained that students would be working in pairs over the course of the semester to learn the basics of sketching and painting.

"The way each of us sees the world is unique," he said. "We need to share our views, but we also need to understand how others see the world. Otherwise, we become myopic, and we never learn a thing. We never grow. Art is about sharing how we see the world. In this class, you're going to do that with another person — ideally, someone who isn't like you. I want you to work together on sketches and paintings that convey something different from anything you would create on your own. In the process, you'll be expanded, and that, I believe, is the true purpose of art."

Olivia liked what she was hearing but was having a hard time understanding how this class was actually going to work.

"Look around you," Nagy said. "Find someone near you who you don't know, someone who doesn't look like you, maybe someone of the opposite sex. Introduce yourself. This will be your partner in this class for the rest of the semester."

A murmur arose from the students. A couple of them laughed. Olivia looked around. The young woman to her left was Indian. The young man to her right was white. She looked at him just as he was looking at her.

"Hello," he said, smiling.

"Hello," she said.

"Would you like to be my partner?" he asked.

"Sure," she said.

"I'm Patrick," he said, extending his hand.

"I'm Olivia," she said, taking it.

Patrick did indeed look different from Olivia. His hair was red and straight. His skin was pale, and he had freckles. He was thin, like Olivia, but much taller.

Once his students had paired up, Nagy instructed them to move to one of the large paper drawing pads set up on easels around the perimeter of the classroom. He told them to sketch whatever they liked, taking turns until their artwork was complete.

Olivia thought it was interesting that Nagy was not more proscriptive or that he didn't start with some type of instruction on how to sketch. He was certainly unlike her other professors.

"How about that one?" Patrick said, pointing to an easel in the back corner of the room.

"Okay," Olivia said.

They walked back to the easel together. A charcoal pencil and an eraser lay in a tray at the base of the drawing pad.

"Would you like to go first?" Patrick asked.

"I'd be happy to," Olivia said. "Any requests?"

"No. Sketch whatever you like. I'll follow your lead," he said, smiling.

"Okay," said Olivia, picking up the pencil.

She slowly drew a slightly rounded line across the bottom of the canvas, leaving a three-inch gap in the middle. In the gap, she drew several curved, winding, vertical lines, flaring out at the top.

"It's a tree," Patrick said.

"Yes, an olive tree," she said.

"Your name," he said.

"How did you know?"

"High school French," he said.

"Francais, eh?" she said, filling in the contour of the trunk and extending it into several thick branches.

"Yeah," he said. "I took it despite my parents' objections."

"Why did they object?"

"They thought it was silly, that I'd never use it."

"Well, I think it's refined."

"Thank you."

"What are you studying?" she asked.

"You mean my major?"

"Yeah," she said, roughing out the foliage, using lots of short, pointed, angular strokes.

"Technically, I'm a business major."

"Technically?"

"Yeah. It's the only way my parents would pay for my college. By the way, that olive tree is looking awesome."

"Thanks. So you don't want to major in business?"

"Hell, no."

"What *do* you want to study?"

"English."

"English? Why?"

"I want to be a poet."

She stopped sketching and turned toward him.

"You want to be a poet, and you're a business major?"

"I know. It sounds crazy."

"Actually," she said, "not so crazy."

"What do you mean?"

She turned back toward the easel and sketched some rocks at the base of the tree and wobbly lines, as the texture of bark, along the trunk.

"I mean I love English," she said. "I wanted to be an English major, but my parents insisted on pre-med. They want me to become a doctor, like them."

"Do you want to be a doctor?"

"Hell, no."

She picked up the eraser from the tray and lightly rubbed

away the thin pencil lines which she had used to guide parts of her drawing.

"There," she said. "An olive tree."

"It looks amazing," he said.

"Well, thank you, Patrick."

"What else?" he asked.

"What do you mean?"

"What else should we draw?"

His question surprised her because she hadn't thought beyond this tree. She had drawn this image all her life. Sometimes she sketched a distant background, but her focus was always on this solitary tree. In her mind, it had become an expression of who she was and how she saw herself in the world, unique and alone.

"Your tree is beautiful, but it looks a little lonely," Patrick said. "I think it needs a friend."

He took a step toward her and held out his hand, his palm open, his fingers outstretched.

Olivia laid the pencil in his hand.

"Thank you," he said, turning toward the drawing pad.

"Olivia," he said, "have you ever seen an olive tree?"

"No, I haven't," she said.

"I have. Hundreds of them. In Provence—in the south of France. I spent a week there last summer."

"Cool."

"I have a rich aunt," he said with a grin. "My trip was a high school graduation gift."

He bent down and began sketching the trunk of a tree next to the one she had drawn.

"You know," he said, "the olive tree is known as the tree of eternity. It's been cultivated for more than 6,000 years. It looks ancient too, green and gray and blue, like the colors in an old movie. I saw rows and rows of olive trees in France. They stand there in the valleys, on the hillsides, in fields thick with red poppies, looking so stately, like ancient sentinels standing guard over the earth. There is an elegance and a serenity to those trees, Olivia, and they're so lovely that it's easy to forget how tough they are too. Did you know olive trees can grow just about anywhere? They're resilient and adaptable. Maybe that's why they've been around for 6,000 years. Maybe we could all learn something from a grove of olive trees."

"I'd like to read your poetry sometime," she said.

"Anytime," he said, roughing out the foliage of his tree. "So why do you want to become an English major?"

Most Special Glasses

Leo adjusted a tiny dial on the black frames of his eyeglasses with one hand and tapped a few keys on his laptop with the other.

"Come on," he pleaded under his breath. "Work."

Leo looked over at Charley, asleep on his little dog bed in the corner of the room.

"How are you today, Charley?"

At the sound of his name, Charley woke up, lifted his head and looked at Leo.

Then Leo pressed a small button on his glasses.

"Confused."

That single word was emitted from a bud nestled in Leo's left ear.

Leo let out a laugh.

"All right!" he said.

Charley tilted his head.

"Confused, huh?" Leo said with a smile. "Well, *you* might be confused, Charley, but everything's becoming clear to me."

At last, Leo thought. He'd designed, redesigned and experimented with this device for nearly three years. Special eyeglasses that could "see" emotions. If Charley was indeed confused, this was the first time Leo's invention had worked so well.

Leo had long dreamed about the wealth and fame his invention could bring him. He knew that, if it worked, he would be celebrated as one of the world's greatest inventors.

But of course, just because his device worked on a dog didn't mean it would work with people. So Leo headed outside to try it among the masses.

He locked his apartment door and headed down the hall to the elevator. He pushed the button, and soon the doors opened. Inside was a young woman with a little boy in a stroller. As Leo stepped in, she smiled a small smile, but her gaze remained fixed on the boy.

As the elevator descended, Leo turned slightly toward the woman and pressed the button on the frame of his glasses.

"Anxious" sounded in his ear, a bit more loudly than "confused" with Charley.

Leo noticed the woman was now watching him out of the corner of her eye and gripping the handles of the stroller tightly. As soon as the elevator came to a stop and the doors opened, she pushed the stroller out fast.

Leo found the episode rather curious, but he was thrilled his device had worked with a human being. He crossed the lobby, pushed open a glass door and stepped out onto the sidewalk, along which people hurried to and fro.

Leo made his way to the nearest street corner, where several people were waiting for the light to change. In front of him stood a tall, handsome, middle-aged man wearing a dark blue suit and holding a slim leather briefcase.

Leo inched just beyond him, then stopped, looked over at the man's face and pressed the button on his glasses.

In his ear, he heard "self doubt."

Just then, the light changed, but the man hesitated, as if he wasn't sure it was indeed safe to cross.

Two blocks later, Leo spotted a young couple coming toward him, walking hand in hand. She wore an easy smile. He looked grim.

When they were almost right in front of him, Leo brought his index finger to his glasses and pressed the button.

"Euphoric" sounded in his ear. Then, more loudly, "afraid."

They need to talk, Leo thought.

Walking on, he came to an old woman sitting alone on a bench, staring into the distance.

Leo stopped and, as nonchalantly as he could, turned her way. Once again, he pressed the button on his glasses.

"Lonely" echoed in his ear, this time loud enough that he wondered if someone else might have heard.

For the rest of that day, Leo walked around the city, observing strangers, pressing the button on his glasses and gleaning emotions. An "ashamed" man. A "jealous" woman. An "insecure" girl.

In some cases, people's expressions gave away their feelings. But in most cases, Leo was surprised. Most people, he observed, hid their feelings well.

And what was completely unexpected was the volume level of the words in Leo's ear. Over the course of the day, he concluded volume must be an indication of the intensity of the emotions he was "seeing" through his device.

That evening, Leo reflected on his experience. He had seen and heard so much, far more than he ever had walking around the city. Through his special glasses, a hidden world had been revealed to him.

Leo was thrilled his invention had finally worked. Yet he was left with an uneasy feeling, as if he had entered a place he didn't belong and uncovered things that were none of his business.

Leo sat at his desk and logged onto his laptop. He tapped a few keys, and up popped a list of the words he'd heard that day. They were all anonymous. Still, he felt he had taken possession of something that wasn't his.

Leo got up, went into his bedroom and looked in his mirror. He was still wearing his special glasses. He brought his finger to the frame and pressed the button. "Wrong" rang in his ear.

Leo took off the glasses and went back into office. The program he'd created was still open on his laptop. With the stroke of a few keys, he deleted it.

Then Leo stood up, picked up the glasses and dropped them onto the hardwood floor. He lifted his right foot and, leaning in, smashed and ground them under his heel.

The whole time, Charley barked furiously. When Leo finally took his foot away from the broken plastic and shattered glass, Charley went silent and looked up at Leo with a kind of smile.

"Happy, boy?" Leo said.

Charley yipped, as if to say yes.

Stepping around the splintered remains of years of hard work and big dreams, Leo grabbed Charley's leash and said, "Let's go for a walk."

Dorothy

I took my groceries from my cart and placed them on the belt.

I watched a young woman at the end of the belt bagging groceries. She was short. Her face was flat, and her head was small. Her eyes were shaped like almonds. Her name tag said Dorothy.

When I was growing up, there was a boy in our neighborhood who looked like this. I never knew his name.

As the cashier scanned my items, I stepped forward to the bagging area.

"May I help you, Dorothy?"

"Sure," she said with a smile.

We stood there, Dorothy and I, side by side, bagging groceries together.

Renewal

Berries

As boys, he and his brother spent a week every summer in northwestern Pennsylvania, where their father grew up. The summers are short there. By July, the blackberry, raspberry and blueberry bushes that cover the wooded hillsides are heavy with fruit.

Their father would take them up into the woods to pick berries. When their bushels were full, they would hike out of the cool woods, into the warm sunshine, and follow trails through meadows of green and gold back to the old house, where their grandmother would make them bowls of mixed berries with cream and sugar.

Those vacations were an adventure because the brothers lived in the city, and there were no hills or meadows or berry bushes there.

Now they're grown men, and they live far from one another. Their lives are busy, and they seldom see each other anymore. Their grandmother is gone. Their father too.

But every summer, they get together. They go to a local market and buy fresh berries. They bring them home, wash them and gently drop them into bowls. Then they pour cream over them and sprinkle them with sugar.

They sit down at the kitchen table, bring spoonfuls of berries to their lips and breathe them in. They open their mouths and close their eyes and let the sweetness and tartness of the berries dance on their tongues, and they go back to the hills of Pennsylvania, to their grandmother's house, to a slower and simpler time.

The Virus

Jayden knew his father was home because he could hear his parents' raised voices downstairs. To him, that sound was like nails on a chalkboard.

He'd been looking at the news. Not that he was into the news. He was just putting off his homework.

He scanned the headlines. Protests. Boycotts. Political vendettas. He couldn't take it and slammed his laptop shut.

He grabbed his backpack, unzipped it and pulled out his notebook. He had only one homework assignment. It was for social studies. He read his notes:

The world seems more divided than ever. Why do you think that is? What do you think we should do about it? What's one thing you can do to help bring people together?

That was the last thing Jayden wanted to think about. He'd grown up with division. He could hear it just then downstairs. The country was divided too, and every day the news made that painfully obvious. Cable news had become a shouting match. Forever wars. Income inequality. Democracy versus autocracy.

The world was not only divided, but filled with rancor. Just thinking about it made Jayden anxious. And now he was supposed to write about it? And come up with something he could do about it?

He got up and lay down on his bed. He closed his eyes and thought about his homework assignment. His whole life, the world had seemed divided. Why? He had no clue. What could bring people together? Maybe an asteroid heading for Earth.

It would take something like that, be thought, some cataclysm, to bring people together. Diplomacy, alliances, even religion hadn't worked. It would have to be a threat, a common enemy. But what kind of threat?

Jayden thought of Covid. To some extent, the pandemic had brought people together, even though how to deal with it had become politicized. What if a virus, maybe even one more lethal than Covid, were to hit?

That'll be my answer, Jayden thought, sitting up. It's not so far-fetched. After all, researchers had said it's only a matter of time before the next pandemic strikes.

Jayden went over to his desk, opened his laptop and created a new document.

Why is the world so divided?
The lack of something that everyone sees as a big threat.

What could bring people together?

Rallying around solutions to a problem that poses an existential threat to all mankind.

There. That wasn't so bad. It's simple, he thought. Fear is the thing that can bring people together. Covid illustrated that. If people feared for their survival, they would act as one.

I can pull this off, Jayden thought. But what about my role in all of it?

"Jayden!" his mother called.

"Yeah?"

"Dinner."

"Okay. Be right down."

His role would have to wait.

Over dinner, while his parents bickered, Jayden thought of a news story he'd read recently about a scientific journal that had gotten into trouble for publishing a paper with fudged data. That gave him an idea.

Back in his bedroom, Jayden went online and found the story — and several others linked to it. They were about the growing number of cases where fake research had been published, cases where *all* the data and the text had been invented from whole cloth, generated with artificial intelligence. They are fake all the way through.

Which led to Jayden's role. Even as a junior in high school, he had developed the digital skills and was familiar enough with AI programs to fabricate a scientific study and post it online.

He knew he might get caught. But so what? He'd say he was doing it as part of a class assignment. Besides, everyone knows teenage boys do crazy things.

But what should his fake research be about? It had to be something specific, something everyone sees as a threat and wants to work together to stop.

Climate change hadn't worked. Nor had the threat of nuclear annihilation. But Covid had worked, at least for a short time.

A new virus, he thought. I'll make up a new virus, even deadlier and more contagious than the coronavirus.

Jayden decided the new virus would be "10 times more dangerous than Covid." Where would it come from? He decided it should be a remote part of the world so it would be hard for people to determine the truth.

Jayden looked up the world's most remote places and landed on the Mamberamo region of Indonesia. It was mainly jungle and not in a country that might be out to get the world.

Jayden figured creating a scientific paper and posting it online would take some time. His social studies homework was due the following day. Of course, he couldn't say anything about his real plan anyway.

So in response to the question about the one thing he could do to help bring people together, Jayden wrote:

Use my digital knowledge and skills to alert people to the danger.

It was a half truth. He just wouldn't be specific about how he was going to use his digital knowledge and skills.

Jayden got an A on his homework assignment. His teacher even wrote: "Great insight."

So he'd checked that box, and there was no need to pursue his idea about a new virus in Indonesia any further.

Except that the bitter division all around him made Jayden more and more uneasy, and the more he thought about it, the more convinced he became that he could not only pull off the virus hoax but that it might *actually* bring people together, at least in Indonesia.

So he went online and found several medical journals published in Indonesia. Then he found and downloaded a dozen scientific papers on Covid.

He mashed up the titles of the medical journals and came up with *The Journal of Indonesian Medicine*. Using AI, he did the same with the scientific papers, creating a "new" research study that revealed a virulent new strain of a Covid-like virus that nearly wiped out a village in the Mamberamo region.

Jayden named it C2. Again using AI, he generated fake news stories and social media posts about the mysterious new virus.

But then he began having second thoughts. He knew that, despite his clever use of digital tools, he could be found out and, if he was, he could be charged with a crime. He wondered if he might even do jail time.

But he had gone into this with both eyes open. The anxiety he felt from the neverending division in the world, and in his daily life, compelled him to do *something*.

Jayden believed what he had written in his homework assignment. He believed in fear as a motivator. But he also believed in people and that they would come together if they had to. That's ultimately how he justified his actions.

At any rate, it was too late now. If things went sideways, at least he'd done something constructive. Or so he hoped.

And so Jayden braced himself and checked the Internet nearly constantly. What he would see he could never have predicted.

Soon researchers from every region of the world began to report similar new strains of a Covid-like virus. What they'd been observing was so concerning that they'd be hesitant to go public for fear of causing a health scare. They were also concerned their home countries might be blamed for the new virus, as China was blamed for Covid-19. But when they saw the Indonesian study, they quickly reported their own findings.

Soon the awful truth became evident to everyone. C2 was much more contagious and deadly than the original strain of the coronavirus. Covid-19 had claimed more than 7,000,000 lives over five years. In just a few months, C2 had quietly killed nearly 1,000,000 people. Jayden's idea that the new virus would be "10 times more dangerous than Covid" wasn't far off.

The world was stunned. There was some finger pointing, but within days, the World Health Organization convened a global summit to set a plan for dealing with the new threat.

Unlike with Covid-19, there would be no piecemeal approach and no political games. The world had learned its lesson. This time, all countries worked together to develop and implement a plan that made sense for the world because the whole world was at dire risk.

It worked. Within a year, new vaccines were developed and distributed to every country in the world. Within two years, C2 was no more.

Ultimately, the new virus claimed the lives of 20 million people. But in that time, the world came together, and the rancorous, corrosive and petty divisions that had plagued daily life simply fell away.

Jayden watched it with awe. No one ever found out he was

behind the Indonesian "study" or even suspected it was a fake. But for the rest of his life, Jayden would know his stunt not only helped save countless lives but showed division doesn't have to be a way of life.

Reconciled

It took me a while to find your keys. I guess I should have known they would be in your purse, but I'd never looked in your purse, and I forgot where you always kept it: on your chair in the dining room. I don't go in there much anymore.

The first thing I did when I got in your Blazer was turn off the radio. NPR. You were always listening to news. Used to drive me crazy.

An opened pack of Virginia Slims lay on the passenger's seat. Your only vice. I wish you had stopped. I picked up the cigarettes and slipped them into my jacket pocket.

I'd never been to Ray's. I was going to take your car to my place, but I know you really liked Ray. Said he always treated you with respect. So I figured I'd let the guy tune up your car one last time before I sell it.

"May I help you?" said a burly man in dark blue coveralls.

His soft voice and careful diction didn't match his body. He was standing behind the counter, wiping his hands with a rag, having just come in from the garage.

"Good morning," I said. "I'm here for a tune-up on my wife's car."

"And you are?"

"Warren Herbert."

"Oh, Mr. Herbert. I'm sorry. I'm Ray," he said, extending his hand.

"Good to meet you," I said, taking it.

"Your wife hasn't been in for a while."

He doesn't know, I thought. I guess I should have told him, but I'd grown weary of telling people.

"Yeah, well, I thought I'd take care of it for her."

"That's very thoughtful," he said. "May I have the keys?"

"Here you go," I said, handing them over. "It's right out there."

"Great. I'll get right on it. Should take me about an hour. You're welcome to wait here. There's a coffee shop across the street. Your wife usually waits over there."

"I'll wait here," I said.

Turning around, I could see why you waited at the coffee shop. The "waiting room" for customers was small, with only three chairs made of hard plastic. A table in the corner was covered with car magazines. Vending machines took up one wall. A black rug, which was more like a mat, covered most of the grey linoleum floor.

I was the only one there. I slipped a dollar bill into a vending machine that dispensed coffee and hot chocolate. Sipping my so-called coffee, I wished I'd gotten the hot chocolate.

I was flipping through one of the magazines when a young woman came in with a small boy. She was quite short with a broad nose, dark complexion and double eyelids. I knew she was from Vietnam. I felt my heart beat faster and the hair on the back of my neck bristle.

"Good morning," she said, walking by me to the counter.

I just nodded.

The young boy was holding her hand. He was looking at me. He had the woman's round face and black hair, but his eyes were bigger and his skin much lighter. His father must be white, I thought.

Ray came in from the garage. I didn't mean to eavesdrop, but I could hear the woman say she was there for a tune-up too.

Seeing the boy holding her hand reminded me of our kids holding your hand when they were little. That seemed so long ago.

The woman came over and sat down two chairs over. The little boy climbed up on the chair between us. He looked up at me.

"William, can you say good morning?" the woman said.

"Good morning," the boy said, leaning against his mother.

"Your son?" I asked.

"Yes."

"And his name is William?"

"Yes."

"That's a good name."

"Thank you. We named him after your President Bill Clinton."

"Is that right?"

"Yes. He re-established relations between our countries."

"You mean with Vietnam."

"Yes. That is my home country."

I just nodded.

"Have you been there?" she asked.

"Yes."

"I'm from Ho Chi Minh City. Maybe you've been there."

"When I was there, it was called Saigon."

"I see," she said.

"Have you been here long?" I asked.

"About five years."

"What brought you here, if you don't mind me asking."

"No, it's fine. I came to the US with my husband."

"Is he American?"

"Yes."

"From around here?"

"No, he's from California, but we moved here because we couldn't afford to live in California."

"I understand."

"This is a nice place, and we wanted to raise a family here."

"I see. Do you have other children?"

"No, just William, so far."

The boy pointed to one of the vending machines and asked his mother if he could have some candy. They stepped over to the machine, and she bought him a Kit Kat bar. Sitting back down, she unwrapped it, and the boy took a big bite.

"What about you?" she asked.

"Pardon me?"

"Do you have children?"

"Oh, yes. We have two."

"How wonderful. We hope to have at least one more too."

I nodded and looked down at William. His mouth was covered with chocolate.

I thought of Jason and Heather as kids, sitting in their high chair, and how their faces were always covered with food. What a mess they made. That bothered me. I didn't have much patience with the kids. You, on the other hand, were patient to a fault. Maybe that's why the kids always preferred you over me.

Maybe I shouldn't be surprised they haven't called me. I guess their thoughts are still with you.

Of course, I haven't called them either. I'm sure you're not happy about that.

But then I had a knack for upsetting you. You sure hated the Blazer. You wanted a RAV4, but I told you I wouldn't have anything made in Asia under our roof. When you said you'd park it in the driveway, I didn't speak to you for days.

William looked up at me and smiled. Now he had chocolate in his hair.

The woman laughed.

"Oh, William!" she said.

She pulled a pack of wet wipes from her purse and cleaned the boy's face and hair as he squirmed.

"Oh, the things we do for our children," she said with a smile.

Jason and Heather used to get so messy at dinner that you would take them straight to the bathtub. I don't remember ever helping you bathe them.

I closed my eyes, leaned my head back against the wall and thought of you. I thought of when we met, when I was still a mess from the war and how you helped me find some peace. You were good for me. You told me not to harbor resentments, that people were more alike than different, that we are all called to love one another. I needed to hear that, and for a while, I believed it. But over time, old memories crept back. They haunted me and hardened me, and I became intolerant again. And not just of people halfway around the world but of the people closest to me. I grew distant from the kids. I grew distant from you. You tried to love me, but I wouldn't let you in, and now it's too late. I'll never see you again. I'm sorry. Maybe it's not too late with Jason and Heather. Maybe I should go see them. Maybe I should try to make things right.

Hearing Ray come back in from the garage, I opened my eyes.

"Mr. Herbert, your wife's car is ready," he said. "No big problems."

I got up and stepped over to the counter.

"What do I owe you?"

"That'll be 50," he said, handing me the keys.

"That's all?"

"Yep. That's our flat rate for routine tune-ups."

I opened my wallet and pulled out a thin stack of crisp twenties, which I'd withdrawn from the ATM that morning. I counted out seven bills and laid them on the counter.

"It's only 50," Ray said.

"Is she getting a tune-up too?" I said in a low voice, pointing to the young woman with my eyes.

"Yes."

"Then this is for both of us, plus a tip."

Ray looked at me and smiled.

"Don't say anything until I'm gone," I said.

"I won't, Mr. Herbert. Thank you. Please give Mrs. Herbert my best."

"Thank you," I said, shaking his hand. "I will."

I turned around. William was on his mother's lap, his head on her chest, his eyes closed.

I looked at the woman's face. It looked like thousands of faces I'd seen before, faces that had made me anxious or angry or afraid so many years ago.

But now I thought of you rocking our children to sleep, and

I realized we are all so much more alike than different and it's never too late to love one another.

"My name is Warren," I said.

She started to reach over her sleeping son, but I said, "It's okay. Let him sleep."

She smiled.

"My name is An," she said softly.

"Good luck to you and your family," I said.

"And to you and yours."

The Grotto

For the first time in decades, Jesse Adler awoke by the sun. His alarm had been one of the countless constructs that had regulated the rhythm of Jesse's life for nearly as long as he could remember.

Now, one by one, those constructs were falling away. Yesterday was his last day at work. His children, Michael and Ashley, now grown, had moved away. His house, once alive with activity, now felt like a museum.

His job, his family, his house. Things such as these had defined Jesse. He had leaned into them, mindlessly at times. Doing so was easy, and it worked. Jesse Adler, the executive, the family man, the guy with the nice house and the cool car. He had it all.

But appearances can be deceiving, like veneer over hollow wood. Outwardly, Jesse's life looked full. But for the most part, his life had been a series of experiences that left him feeling empty.

Jesse blamed no one but himself. He knew it was his fault that his job wasn't more satisfying, his marriage wasn't more fulfilling and his children weren't more affectionate toward their father. And yet what could he do about it now?

Now, on the first morning of his retirement, Jesse was alone. His wife Laura had left for work before he awoke.

Sipping his coffee, he looked out his kitchen window into his large backyard — verdant, manicured, picturesque — and decided to go out and walk around.

Jesse stepped across his brick patio and out into the grass. Some of the trees and bushes were unfamiliar to him. He hadn't worked in his yard for many years. A landscaping service took care of it.

He approached an English garden that spanned nearly half of the rear of his wooded lot. He liked looking out at the flowers from his patio but hadn't seen them up close in years.

Now he surveyed the well designed mosaic of roses, lavender, peonies, phlox, dianthus, hollyhocks, hydrangeas, sweet peas, clematis and boxwoods. He remembered the names from when he worked with his mother in her garden as a boy. That was so long ago, when he used to get his hands dirty.

When he got to the end of the garden, Jesse noticed how the ground sloped down and the nursery had built a low stone wall to keep the bed level and prevent erosion. He couldn't recall seeing that wall. Now, staring down at it, he remembered something he'd long forgotten.

When Jesse was a boy, his father used to go on retreats at a church center set on many acres of land, much of it wooded. The Adlers had only one car, so Jesse's mother would drive his father to and from those retreats. Jesse and his younger brother rode along.

Afterwards, Jesse's father took his family on short hikes on the church center property. They always went to a large grotto that had been built into a hillside in the woods. It was made of layers of stacked stones. Rows of candles filled the small cavern. There,

Jesse and his brother would light candles as their parents recited the names of loved ones.

Jesse loved the whole experience: holding the long, wooden matches, watching the candle wicks catch flame and imagining that somehow this ritual was helping the people for whom their prayers were being offered.

Lighting those candles gave Jesse a feeling of peace and connectedness he hadn't known since. Now discovering that stone wall in his backyard brought those memories and that feeling back.

Jesse looked across his wide garden. At the other end was a hill. He walked down to it. He stood there a long time, studying the slope of the land, and got an idea.

———

"A grotto?" Laura said that evening over dinner.

"Yeah," Jesse said. "Just a small one."

"Are you going to put a statue in it?" she said sarcastically.

"No, just candles."

"Candles?"

"Yeah."

"Why?" Laura said, looking at Jesse like she was worried about him.

"Do you really want to know?"

"Yes."

"Okay. When I was a kid, I used to go to a grotto in the woods with my parents and my brother. Joe and I lit candles there. It was such a great experience. I can't really describe it. Anyway, I walked out to our English garden this morning, and when I saw the stone wall at one end, it reminded me of that grotto. There's a pretty good-sized hill at the other end. I think I can dig it out and make a little grotto."

Laura wore a look of disbelief.

"Is this what you're going to do in your retirement?" she said.

His face fell.

"I thought you might be more supportive."

"Look, Jesse, it's your retirement. You've earned it. You can do anything you want. I just didn't think you'd start by trying to relive your childhood."

"I'm not trying to relive my childhood, Laura. I just thought it might be something nice for all of us."

"All of us?"

"Yeah, you, me and the kids."

She laughed a small, derisive laugh.

"Come on, Jesse. Do it if you want, but don't do it for us."

"Okay," he said, sounding defeated. "I'll do it for myself."

She rolled her eyes.

"Are you going to have the nursery build it?"

"No, I thought I'd try to do it myself."

"Good Lord."

She shook her head, got up and brought her plate and silverware over to the sink.

"I'm starting to worry about you," she said, looking back at him as she left the room.

Jesse sat there and finished his dinner in silence.

It took him a week to dig a semicircle in the hill. He knew he could have rented a mini dozer and probably got the job done in a hour. But there was something about digging it out with a shovel and a mattock that felt right. It was hard work, maybe the hardest physical labor he'd ever done. But he found it strangely satisfying.

Each evening, Laura came out to inspect. At first, she grumbled and took potshots. That didn't surprise him. But by the end of the week, watching the contours of the grotto take shape and seeing her husband covered with mud and drenched in sweat, her disposition seemed to change. She managed to throw him a compliment and even bring him a cold beer.

That *did* surprise him. Over the years, Laura had grown distant from Jesse. She was hard on him. He didn't blame her. He was hardly ever around, and he knew it was Laura who, for the most part, raised their kids. She even stepped away from her career for five years and stayed home. He knew she resented him for it and that he should have been home more, but he wasn't.

And when he was home, Jesse wasn't much help. It was clear to him the kids preferred their mother, and he gave up trying to earn their affection.

All the while, Laura bought nicer and more expensive things. Jesse thought it was her attempt to fill a void. He didn't like it, but he never challenged her. He knew she'd give him no quarter if he had.

Jesse was on a fast track at work. At first, the promotions lit him up. But over time, his responsibilities became so great that he could hardly take a day off. He felt beholden to the demands of executive positions he had been clear he wanted and worked hard to earn.

Constructs. His job, his family, his affluent lifestyle: these were the things that both defined Jesse's life and kept him from being happy.

Sometimes he wished things could be the way they were when he and Laura first met. They had little money but were madly in love. Now, 30 years later, they slept in separate bedrooms. Some days, they barely acknowledged each other.

But when Laura had brought him that beer when he was digging out the grotto, Jesse noticed something in the way she looked at him he hadn't seen in a long time. He held her gaze, and he felt she *liked* what she saw. For the first time in a long time, she seemed interested in him.

———

Jesse dumped most of the dirt and clay he removed in the woods. He pulled out the larger rocks and tossed them into a pile. He would need much more stone for the grotto, but he liked the idea that at least some of it was "indigenous."

When he was finished digging, Jesse estimated how many stones he would need. He then went to the nursery that had done all his landscaping and picked out the type of natural stone he had in mind. He bought several cubic yards of it and a few bags of concrete mix and arranged for delivery.

It took him two weeks to do all the stone work. He used a string level, set the stones in place one layer at a time and made sure everything looked just right before removing each of the stones, carefully troweling in wet concrete and setting the stones firmly in place.

One evening, Laura came out and asked if she could help.

"Sure," Jesse said. "But you'll get dirty."

"I don't mind," she said with a big smile.

Seeing his wife smile that way and knowing she wanted to help with a project she had initially derided made Jesse's heart feel light.

That weekend, Jesse and Laura finished the grotto. Stepping back, Jesse said, "Now all we need is some candles."

"How about a bench too?" Laura said.

"A bench?"

"Yeah. I'd like to be able to sit here with you and enjoy it."

Jesse felt a little dizzy, like he did when he was first falling in love with Laura.

The following day, they went to the nursery and picked out a bench. The frame was cast iron. It was heavy, came in a big, flat box and required assembly. They brought it home in Laura's SUV, carried it out to the patio together and worked together patiently and without a cross word to assemble it.

The following afternoon, they went out and bought a case of votive candles, a box of clear glass holders and some long, wooden matches. When they got home, they placed a dozen or so candles on the floor of the grotto and took turns lighting them. With each candle, they said the name of a loved one, including their own names.

Then they went over to the bench and sat down. Jesse put his arm around his wife, and they sat there well into the evening, talking about things they hadn't mentioned in years. It was as if the candlelight had opened them up.

That night, for the first time in years, Jesse and Laura slept together.

Over breakfast the next morning, Laura said, "So you said you were building the grotto for all of us."

"Yeah."

"Why don't you invite the kids to come home and see it?"

"Okay," he said.

After breakfast, Jesse called Michael and Ashley and invited them to come visit. They seemed surprised and asked if everything was okay. He assured them it was. That Friday evening, they both came home.

After dinner, holding hands, Jesse and Laura brought them out back and proudly showed them the grotto.

"We built it together," Jesse said.

"Well, you did the hard work," Laura said. "I just pitched in."

Jesse and Michael carried two Adirondack chairs out from the patio and placed them at the ends of the bench.

When they were getting the chairs, Ashley said to her mother, "So when did you and Dad start holding hands?"

"You noticed," Laura said, blushing.

The four of them went to the grotto and took turns lighting candles and saying the names of loved ones. Then they sat back and took in the warm glow of the candles.

Jesse told them about his experience at the retreat center when he was a boy and how, in lighting candles at the grotto there, he had felt such peace and connectedness with his loved ones.

"I wanted to recreate that experience," he said, "and share it with you."

"We're glad you did, Dad," Ashley said.

"Yeah," Michael said. "Thank you."

And then, under the outstretched arms of an old oak, the Adlers watched shadows from the candlelight dance across the stone walls of the grotto, and they began catching up.

The Garden

The old man raised his hoe high in the air and brought it down, striking the thick, encrusted soil with all his might. He grimaced and moaned as a pain shot through his arms and into his shoulders and back.

But an even deeper pain tore at his heart. Decades after his offense, he still bore the guilt of it. He could not let it go.

He had reserved this section of the garden for carrots and cucumbers, the last vegetables he planted every year. The earth here had been untouched through the winter and spring. It was uneven, full of clods and covered with the blanched and shriveled carcasses of last year's vines.

He knew preparing this rough patch for carrot seeds and cucumber seedlings would take a day's hard work, maybe more. It was only morning, and he was already withering under the June sun.

He felt a tightness in his chest and a stabbing pain in his stomach. He was panting, trying to catch his breath. He felt dizzy, like he was going to fall down. *I'm having a heart attack,* he thought.

What if this is it? I'm still not rid of my great sin. Will I burn in Hell? Or will God forgive me?

He dropped the hoe and fell to his knees.

"I'm sorry, Lord," he mumbled as he keeled over onto the dry, hard earth.

Two years earlier

He pulled her forward slightly with his right hand and stuffed the pillow down behind her with his left.

"How's that?" he asked.

"Better," she said softly, sitting up best she could. "Thank you."

"What do you feel like eating tonight?" he asked.

"Nothing really."

"But you have to eat something, Marie."

"Okay, Joe, she said, looking over the tray in front of her. "How about a little of that pudding?"

He got up from his chair next to her hospital bed, reached over and pulled the plastic wrap off a small bowl of chocolate pudding. Then he picked up a spoon, scooped up a little pudding and brought it to her lips. She leaned forward and opened her mouth, and he slowly inserted the spoon. She closed her mouth, and he gently pulled out the spoon.

"How is it?" he asked.

"Very good," she said.

"Another bite?"

"No," she said. "Not right now. I think I'd like to rest."

She leaned back against her pillows and sighed. He pushed the table down toward her feet, then sat down.

"Joe," she said, closing her eyes.

"Yes?"

"I have something I must tell you."

"What is it, Marie?"

He noticed a tear rolling down her cheek.

"Are you okay?" he asked.

"Joe," she said, opening her eyes and looking at him, "I did something wrong, something very wrong, years ago."

Joe sat quietly with his hands folded on his lap.

"Oh, Joe," she said. "I was unfaithful to you. It happened only once. It was many years ago, and I feel awful for having done it. I regretted it as soon as I did it. I was foolish, but I knew what I was doing. I knew it was wrong, but I did it anyway. I should have told you long ago, but I couldn't bring myself to do it. I was too ashamed, and I was afraid you might think I had stopped loving you. But I've never stopped loving you, Joe. I'm sorry. I'm so sorry. Can you forgive me?"

He took her hand.

"Yes, Marie," he said. "I forgive you."

"Thank you, Joe," she said with a faint smile. "I love you so very much."

She closed her eyes and fell asleep.

"Marie," he said, leaning in. "There is something I must tell you too."

But she did not wake up. She slept with a look of peace on her face, as if she were no longer suffering.

He held her hand a long time and stayed by her side all night. When he awoke in the morning, she had passed.

"Morning, old man," someone said.

Joe opened his eyes. He looked up at the white ceiling. He wondered where he was and who was talking to him.

"You're alive, still on earth, not in heaven."

Joe looked over in the direction of the voice. There, in a recliner, sat Andy Stewart, his best friend. He was smiling.

"Where am I?" Joe asked. "And what are you doing here?"

"You're in the hospital," Andy said. "And I'm here because, apparently, I'm the only person in the world who cares about you."

"Son of a bitch," Joe said. "What's going on? Why am I here? How long have I been here?"

"You had a heart attack," Andy said. "A bad one. They call it the widow maker."

"Well, it's a little late for that."

"Funny. You almost died, you bastard. If your next-door neighbor hadn't seen you lying in your garden and called 911, you'd be dead now."

"My garden," Joe said. "That's right. What day is it?"

"It's Tuesday."

"So I've been out all night?"

"Yeah. They brought you in yesterday afternoon. They put in a stent, near your heart. Saved your life. I guess they drugged you up pretty good because the nurse just told me you slept all night."

"When did you get here?"

"About an hour ago."

"What time is it?"

"A little after eight."

Joe closed his eyes.

"So I didn't die," he said.

"No, Joe, you didn't die. Are you disappointed?"

"Not really, Andy. But I was kind of curious about where I would have ended up."

Two days later, Andy brought Joe dinner at home.

"Do you want to join me?" Joe asked.

"Do I have to?" Andy said.

"Did you bring enough for both of us?"

"Yeah."

"Great. Let's eat in the kitchen."

They stepped into the kitchen. Andy had brought two spaghetti dinners. Joe got out plates, forks and napkins and put them on the table. Andy pulled plastic containers of spaghetti out of a bag and slid the pasta onto the plates.

"What would you like to drink?" Joe asked.

"Are you allowed wine?"

"Probably not," Joe said. "Chianti okay?"

"Yeah."

Joe uncorked a bottle and poured generous amounts of wine into two glasses. He brought them over to the table and sat down across from Andy.

"To your health," Andy said, raising his glass.

"Thank you," Joe said, clinking his glass. "Thank you for dinner."

Over dinner, Andy said, "So Joe, I have question for you."

"Shoot."

"Why are you always so miserable?"

"Well, in case you don't remember, I had a heart attack a few days ago."

"I don't mean that. I mean before that."

"Well, maybe it's because I lost my wife."

"No. You were miserable long before Marie died."

"You're serious?"

"Look, I've known you for 50 years. You haven't been yourself for the past 30."

"And you're asking me now?"

"Yeah, I'm asking you now."

"And you really want to know?"

"Yeah, I really want to know."

Joe pushed his plate aside and took a drink of wine.

"About 30 years ago, I committed a great sin."

"Thirty years ago? And you're just getting around to telling me?"

"Well, you never asked until now."

"Go on," Andy said, sipping his wine.

"I was at work late one night. I was in my office. I thought everybody had gone home, but there was a knock at my door. I looked up, and standing there was a beautiful young woman. I mean a knockout. She looked familiar. Then I realized she worked for me. She was on my team. Her name was Kimberly. I didn't know her very well. Anyway, she apologized for coming by so late in the day but asked if I could give her some advice with a project. I said yes, and she came in and sat down."

"Oh, boy," said Andy.

"Yeah. It started out okay. She slid a draft recommendation across my desk. She wanted my thoughts on it. I read it. The whole time, she was looking at me. When I was done, I gave her my reaction and made a few suggestions. She was taking notes, seemed very interested in what I was saying. When I was finished, she thanked me and asked if there was anything she could do for me. Andy, I must have been a fool but, until that moment, the thought that she would want anything to do with me never crossed my mind. I mean I was old enough to be her father."

"What did you say?"

"I don't remember exactly. Probably something like, 'Keep

doing a great job.' Well, the next thing I know, she saying she'd like to pay me back right now. By then, I knew what was happening, but she was so sexy, I felt powerless. She got up and turned off the light. Then she came over, behind my desk, and sat on my lap and started kissing me. I knew it was all wrong, but I kissed her back. We started making out, and the next thing I know, we're doing it on my desk."

"You're making this up, right?" Andy said. "You read about this in *Penthouse* or something, right?"

Joe closed his eyes and lowered his head.

"Joe? Are you okay?"

Joe looked up. He had tears in his eyes. Andy had never seen him this way.

"I screwed up, Andy. I screwed up big time."

"I'm sorry, Joe."

"Yeah. I'm sorry too."

"So what did you do after that?" Andy asked.

"Well, first of all, I called Kimberly to my office the next day and told her I was sorry for what had happened the night before. She said she wasn't. I told her I was serious, that this could never happen again. I told I thought it was best if she no longer worked on my team. 'But I don't report to you directly,' she said. I told her that didn't matter. I offered to make arrangements to have her assigned to a different division. She asked if that would hurt her career. I told her it wouldn't. For a moment, I worried that she might file a complaint or something. But she said okay. Thank God. I talked to a couple of people later that day, including Kimberly's boss, and we came up with a move that made sense for her. Kimberly's boss told her about it, as if it were all his idea, and she was all for it."

"Did you ever work with her again?"

"No. I followed her career for a while. She seemed to be doing just fine, getting promoted on time, all of that. The buzz about her was good, and I assumed she was happy. Honestly, I didn't want to ask too many questions."

"I can understand why," Andy said.

"At some point, I knew I would be okay at work, that this incident wasn't going to ruin my career, that there wouldn't be a scandal, that I was going to be able to retire. And Kimberly must have never talked about what happened because I never heard any rumors."

"You're lucky," Andy said.

"In a way, yes. But I did something terrible, Andy. I committed a mortal sin, and I've carried that sin around with me for 30 years."

"Do you think Marie ever suspected anything?"

"No," Joe said. Then he proceeded to tell Andy about Marie's deathbed confession.

"Good lord," Andy said. "Why didn't you tell her then?"

"I tried, but she fell asleep as soon as she told me and never woke up."

"Andy, you screwed up, but that was 30 years ago, and unless you're not telling me everything, it happened only one time."

"Yeah, just once."

"And you're clearly sorry for what you did."

"Yeah."

"Well, then, why are you telling me all this now?"

Joe held his glass of wine in both of his hands and raised it to eye level, his elbows resting on the table, and stared into it.

"Because I'm afraid, Andy. I'm afraid this sin is going to kill me and that, when it does, I'm going to burn in Hell for what I've done."

"Joe, you've got to let this go."

"Let it go? Andy, do you have any idea how this sin weighs on me?"

"Not exactly. But I can see it's tearing you up."

Joe sat his wine glass down on the table and looked up at Andy.

"Do you believe in Hell?"

"I don't know. I mean I used to, when I was young. But now, I'm not so sure."

"Well, I believe in it."

"And you think you're going there because of this one mistake?"

"It's a pretty big mistake, Andy."

"Are you sorry for what you did, Joe?"

"Absolutely."

"Well, don't you think God knows that? Don't you think he's forgiven you?"

"I don't know."

"Well, let's just say he has. How would you feel then?"

"I'd still feel terrible."

"Why?"

"Because my sin wasn't against God. It was against Marie. We made a promise to each other, and I broke it."

"She broke it too, Andy."

"I know. But it's not the same."

"How is it not the same?"

"Because I forgave her."

"So you want Marie to forgive you? Is that what you want?"

"Yeah, I guess it is. But now it's too late."

"Is it?"

"What do you mean?"

"I mean what's keeping you from asking Marie now? She can hear you."

Joe blinked.

"Maybe you're right."

"Actually, I don't think I am."

"What are you talking about? You just told me to ask Marie to forgive me."

"Yeah, and then what? Will you feel forgiven?"

"Of course. Why wouldn't I?"

"Because I don't think it's Marie's forgiveness that will set you free."

"Well, then, whose it is, Andy?" Joe said, sounding irritated.

"It's yours, Joe. You need to forgive yourself."

Joe thought about this for a moment. It sounded too simple. *If it were that simple, I would have thought of it long ago. This is not the advice I need. Maybe I shouldn't have confided in Andy. I'm looking for a way to save my soul, and he comes up with this crap?*

"I'm tired," Joe said, standing up. "I think I'll get to bed early. Thanks again for dinner."

"Okay, Joe," Andy said, getting up. "Can I help you clean up?"

"No, thanks. I'll get it."

"Okay. Get some rest."

Joe walked him to the front door.

"Good night," he said, extending his hand.

"Good night," Andy said, taking it.

Joe cleaned up the kitchen, then poured himself another glass of wine and went into the family room. He sat down on the sofa, where he used to sit with Marie and drink coffee in the morning.

He thought about when they first met, when he began to fall in love with her. He thought about the first time she invited him over to dinner with her family and how nervous he was and how she put him at ease by asking him to go out back with her after dinner. They walked into her backyard and sat on a bench next to her father's garden. It was a large garden, bordered on three sides by apple trees.

Marie asked Joe if he would like an apple. He said yes, and she got up and picked one for him. He bit into it. It was juicy and bursting with flavor. Apple juice ran down his chin which made her laugh, and she wiped it off with her fingers. It was the first time she had ever touched his face. He would never forget the feel of her fingers on his face.

Forgive myself?   How ridiculous. It's Marie I've sinned against. It's her forgiveness I seek.

He finished his wine and went to bed.

Joe woke up the next morning, went downstairs and made himself a cup of coffee.

He decided to drink it on the patio. Sitting there, he looked out over his backyard. He looked out on his large garden, bordered on three sides by apple trees, which he had planted for Marie 40 years earlier. She had loved her father's backyard and asked Joe to create the same for her. It took him years, but he did so gladly.

He walked with his coffee to the edge of the garden and sat down on a bench he had built there. He used to sit there with Marie. Sometimes they sat there together in the morning, sometimes in the evening and sometimes to rest after working in the garden. They had always worked in the garden together. Now he felt so off-balance working in it alone.

He looked up at the apple trees. They were beginning to bear fruit. He sat his coffee mug down on the bench, got up and walked over to one of the trees. Its branches were filled with apples, partly red and partly still green. He reached up and pulled one down.

He bit into it. It was surprisingly juicy for being so early in the season. Juice dripped down his chin. He imagined Marie wiping it with her fingers. But there was no one there, so he brought his fingers to his chin and wiped the juice away.

Then he did something he had not done in a very long time. He rested his fingers and the palm of his hand on the side of his face. He closed his eyes and thought only about the feeling in both his fingers and his face. To his fingers, his face felt warm and perfect, and to his face, his fingers felt like they belonged to the hand of God.

He opened his eyes and looked at the garden and saw it not as a thing to be tamed, like a wayward child, but as part of creation and, as such, perfect and beloved just as it was, and he felt light and free and forgiven.

Live Oak

Chiara always loved trees. Her earliest memories were of watching her brothers climb a big sycamore in their backyard.

She remembered them scaling it by grabbing hold of the huge truck and stepping up little boards their father had nailed up. She remembered them disappearing into the branches and staying up there for what seemed a very long time, calling her name.

They knew she couldn't climb up after them. She was too young. Even when she grew, Chiara wasn't able to climb that tree or any other for that matter. She could never manage to scale a tree trunk.

But one day when she was eight, Chiara came upon a massive oak in the woods near her house. It was unlike any tree she had ever seen. Its lowest limbs nearly touched the ground, extending from its great trunk like giant arms.

Chiara leaned over one, belly high. She swung her left leg up over it and sat up, straddling it. Then she crouched on the enormous limb, grabbed a sturdy branch above her and pulled herself up.

For the first time, she was climbing a tree! Exhilarated, she made it all the way to the top, where she looked out over all the other trees, even a few sycamores.

Chiara felt dizzy but safe in the arms of the rock-solid tree. She felt as if she had been lifted up to the sky. She imagined herself as an angel, looking down on all of creation.

When she got home, Chiara told her mother about the special tree she had found.

"That's a live oak," her mother said.

"A live oak? Aren't all oak trees alive?"

"Yes, but a live oak stays green all winter."

"How does it do that?"

"Somehow it holds onto its leaves and drops them in the spring."

Chiara thought about telling her brothers. Maybe they'd want to climb this special tree too. But they'd become teenagers, and they'd lost interest in climbing trees.

But Chiara never lost interest in that live oak. She climbed it as a teenager. It was the last thing she did before she left home and moved away.

Now Chiara is old, and her parents and brothers are gone. Every summer, she goes back into the woods near her old house. The live oak is still there. Slowly, cautiously, careful to not disturb any leaves, Chiara climbs to the top.

She is mindful this is the only tree she has ever climbed. She remembers the day she first saw it. She wonders if she found it or it found her.

Chiara, now old like the tree, holds fast to its branches. She feels dizzy but safe. She looks out over all creation and imagines she's an angel.

The Letter

Shaking, sweating and spent, the woman gripped the sides of her hospital bed, bore down and pushed with her last ounce of strength. Her tiny baby, halfway out of her body, slipped out completely, into her doctor's waiting hands.

"It's a girl," her doctor said.

"Oh, a girl!" the woman cried, looking down at her baby, then over at her husband, tears rolling down her cheeks.

"Little Michelle," her husband said, taking his wife's hand.

"Here she is," her doctor said, gently laying the baby on her mother's chest.

"She's beautiful," her mother sobbed.

"She sure is," her father said.

After about a minute, the doctor said, "I need to cut the umbilical cord, Anna."

"Okay," the woman said.

"Already?" her husband asked.

"Yes," the doctor said. "Once we do that, we can get your daughter cleaned up, and you can hold her again."

A nurse picked up the baby, holding her away from her mother, and the doctor applied a clamp to the umbilical cord. Then she applied another clamp a couple of inches away from the first. Anna looked down as she picked up a scissors.

"Will this hurt?" she asked.

"No," the doctor said. "Neither you nor the baby will feel a thing."

The nurse was holding the baby facing Anna. As the doctor got ready to cut the cord, the baby opened her eyes and looked directly into Anna's eyes, as if she could see her mother.

"Wait," said Anna, holding up her hand.

The doctor stopped and looked at her.

"Wait, just one more moment," Anna said.

All the while, the baby continued to look up at her mother. Anna knew her doctor must cut the cord. But she felt a special bond with her newborn daughter, a bond she knew she would never know again, and she wanted it to last just a moment longer.

Anna and Michelle held each other's gazes. It was as if mother and daughter both knew they must revel in this moment before the tie that had bound them together would be severed.

Michelle would be Anna and James' only child. Maybe this added to Michelle's need for connection.

She was close to both her parents, but especially her mother. Anna worked from home before her daughter was born, and she continued working from home throughout her childhood. At home, Anna was always at her daughter's side. She was there when she learned to crawl and took her first steps. She taught her to play the piano and ride a bike. She put her on the bus on her first day of school.

In school, Michelle made friends easily. She loved to spend time with her classmates and make new friends. Like all kids, she loved to play at recess. But her favorite thing to do was simply talk with one or two friends at a time.

Michelle had 14 first cousins. None of them lived nearby. She saw them at the holidays and wrote them letters through the year. They weren't used to writing letters, but most of them wrote back to Michelle. She treasured their correspondence, which she kept in a cardboard box under her bed.

In 1994, when Michelle turned 12, email was becoming popular. Her parents had a desktop computer at home, and they let Michelle use it. She got her own email address. She was excited by the idea of being able to connect so easily with her friends and family members.

At the same time, she missed getting their letters. She missed holding them in her hands and seeing their unique handwriting, which seemed so much more personal than an email message.

By the late 1990s, when Michelle was a teenager, social media emerged. She was one of the first to join Six Degrees. Her universe of "friends" expanded dramatically overnight. She also signed up for AOL Instant Messenger, which allowed her to "chat" with anyone in her network in real time. She now had her own computer and was spending hours online every day.

In college, Michelle sent emails to her mother nearly every day. By her senior year, though, she didn't have to because she and her mother were now "friends" on Facebook.

Michelle made new friends in college, though far fewer than she had in high school or even grade school. Everyone seemed so busy now. Everyone was spending so much time online.

Michelle majored in sociology and went to work after graduation for a non-profit whose mission was to help underprivileged kids in the inner city. However, Michelle spent most of her time not with kids but filling out forms. Frustrated, she left after six months.

While looking for a new job, Michelle found herself spending more and more time on social media sites, especially Facebook. She followed many of her friends from high school and college. They all looked great, and their lives seemed so perfect. She found herself posting fewer updates and photos of her own. She felt bad about not having a job or a boyfriend and not being able to post photos from some exciting city or exotic adventure.

And so she began to hold back in her online communication. She stopped posting regular updates on Facebook, and for the first time since she began doing email, she didn't feel obliged to respond to nearly every message.

But this made Michelle feel even worse because she began to feel disconnected from people, and for her, this was the worst feeling of all.

* * *

One day, while she was preparing a cover letter for her resume, Michelle's smartphone rang. *Funny,* she thought. *Nobody calls me anymore.*

She looked at her phone. "Mom" and her mother's photo flashed up on the screen. Michelle picked up her phone.

"Hi, Mom," she said.

"Hi, honey."

Her mother sounded downbeat.

"How are you?" Michelle asked.

"Okay."

"Just okay? Is everything all right?"

"Yes. I was just calling to see if you'd like to come over for dinner tonight."

"Sure. What time?"

"How about six?"

"Sounds great. Can I bring anything?"

"No, thanks. I was thinking about making chicken pot pie and mashed potatoes."

"Mmmm. You know that's still my favorite."

"I was hoping so. I'll see you at six then."

"Sounds good. Oh, will Dad be there?"

"Yes. In fact, he's home right now."

"He is? He's not at work?"

"Uh, no. He decided to take the afternoon off."

"Oh. Good. See you tonight."

"I love you, Michelle."

"Thanks, Mom. I love you too."

Michelle hung up, wondering why her mother sounded distant and her father, a notorious workaholic, would be taking the afternoon off.

Michelle's mother and father seemed unusually quiet over dinner.

"Would you like some ice cream?" her mother asked. "I've got chocolate chip."

"Sure," said Michelle.

Her mother got up, taking their plates with her into the kitchen. Michelle picked up the silverware and followed her.

"Mom," she said. "What's wrong?"

Her mother placed the plates in the sink, turned around and leaned against the counter. She looked at Michelle and started crying, burying her face in her hands.

"Mom," Michelle said, stepping over and putting her arms around her. "Are you okay?"

"No. I have breast cancer."

Anna fought hard to beat the cancer. She had surgery and underwent chemotherapy and radiation. But the cancer, already advanced when her doctor discovered it, spread to her lungs, liver and brain.

She lasted 11 months. Michelle hardly left her side throughout, helping her at home, taking her to her appointments, staying with her in the hospital and tending to her at home.

She was with her at the end.

"Michelle," her mother whispered, lying in bed, her eyes closed.

"Yes, Mom," she said, holding her hand.

"I will always be with you," she whispered.

Michelle was leaning in, a foot from her mother's face. Michelle waited for her to say something else or draw another breath, but her face remained motionless. Michelle looked down at her chest. It didn't move. She squeezed her mother's hand. It was limp and lifeless.

"Oh, Mom," Michelle moaned. "I will always be with you too."

Her father, who had been standing behind Michelle, put his hands on her shoulders.

"She loved you so much," he said, his tears falling on her head.

"Oh, Dad," Michelle said, turning and wrapping her arms around him.

After her mother's funeral, Michelle moved in with her father. She could no longer bear living alone or the thought of her father living alone.

She wished she had moved back home sooner, when her mother was ill. She didn't because she wanted to give her parents their own space. But the three of them had always been close, and now she wondered if she had made the right choice.

One morning that spring, her father at work, Michelle went for a walk. She walked down the sidewalks of her childhood to a park where she had spent countless hours as a girl. Her mother had often taken her there.

She sat on a bench overlooking a pond and watched a flock of Mallards swimming around. She spotted a female, with mottled brown feathers, leading a raft of brown and yellow ducklings. The hen stayed close to the flock, and the ducklings followed close behind wherever she swam.

It made Michelle think of her mother and how, as a girl, she followed her everywhere. She wondered if her mother ever minded that. If she did, she never showed it. She always seemed happy to have Michelle nearby.

Michelle closed her eyes. She could hear her mother saying, "I will always be with you." She could feel her mother's presence, as if she were sitting right beside her. She opened her eyes, half expecting to see her. But all she saw were the Mallards.

She watched the ducklings follow their mother out of the water and onto the grassy bank. She missed her mother so very much, and she began to cry.

Michelle went home and decided to bake some cookies for her father. She seldom baked cookies anymore. Growing up, though, she had baked cookies with her mother nearly every Saturday morning. Now she pulled out the cookie sheet, the glass bowl and the rubber spatula they had used.

Michelle's favorite cookie was chocolate chip with peanut butter mixed in and M&Ms on top. She looked around for M&Ms but couldn't find any, though she did find a bag of chocolate chips and jar of peanut butter in the pantry.

She had a plate of warm cookies waiting for her father when he got home from work that evening.

"Someone's been baking," he said as he walked into the family room from the garage.

"I made cookies," Michelle said from the kitchen.

Her father said nothing more. She peeked into the family room. He was sitting on the sofa, with his head in his hands.

"Dad, are you okay?" she asked.

"Yeah," he said, looking up and wiping away his tears. "The smell of cookies reminds me of Mom."

"Oh, Dad," she said, walking over and embracing him. "I'm sorry."

"It's okay," he said. "She loved baking cookies."

Over dinner, her father told Michelle that, in recent years, her mother had baked several dozen cookies a week.

"Several dozen?" Michelle said.

"Not for me," he said, smiling. "For the prisoners."

"The prisoners?"

"Yeah, she baked the cookies on Saturday, then brought them to church on Sunday. She gave them to Mrs. Rigby, who's charge of our parish prison ministry."

"I had no idea," Michelle said. "Did Mom go visit the prisoners herself?"

"No," her father said. "She didn't feel comfortable doing that. But she certainly baked them a lot of cookies over the years.

Maybe you'd like to get involved."

"I don't know," Michelle said.

"Well, if you like, you could bake a few more dozen cookies tomorrow and bring them to church on Sunday," her father said.

"Maybe I will."

"Just leave the dozen you baked today for me," her father said, smiling.

———

"Would you like to go with me to deliver these this afternoon?" asked Mrs. Rigby.

She had long, gray hair and kind, blue eyes. She sat behind a card table in the foyer of the church. Clear, plastic bags of cookies were heaped on top of it, and a paper sign marked *Prison Ministry* hung from the front.

"No one else has signed up this week, and I could use the help," Mrs. Rigby said.

"What would that entail?" Michelle asked.

"Well, if you like, you can help me give them to the prisoners."

"How does that work?"

"Well, we usually give cookies to about 20 prisoners every Sunday."

"Do you talk with them?" Michelle asked.

"Sometimes," Mrs. Rigby said. "Some of them want to talk. Some of them just want to take the cookies."

"What do you talk about?"

"Whatever's on their minds."

Mrs. Rigby could see a look of uncertainty, maybe even concern, on Michelle's face.

"It can take a while to get used to it," she said. "If you come with me today, you don't have to meet with the prisoners. Or maybe you just want to meet with just one."

"I think I could meet with one," Michelle said.

"Good," Mrs. Rigby said. "Let's meet here at two o'clock. I'll be happy to drive."

"Are they dangerous?" Michelle asked as they drove to the prison.

"We've been doing this for more than 10 years, and we've never had an issue," Mrs. Rigby said. "Most of them are just grateful to have someone to talk to. And, of course, they love the cookies."

A guard led Michelle down a hallway to a door. He opened it.

"You can wait in here, miss," he said.

"Thank you," she said.

She stepped inside. The room was small. The walls were white. She detected the faint scent of a cleaning product. A large mirror covered much of one wall. On the other side of the room was another door. In the center were two gray, metal chairs facing each other. Otherwise, the room was empty.

She stepped over to one chair, took hold of the top and slid it slightly away from the other chair. It was aluminum. She sat down, setting her bag of cookies on her lap.

In that moment, she thought of her mother. She wondered why she had never mentioned baking cookies for these prisoners. She wondered why she had never come there to give them the cookies herself. She wondered if her mother had known something that she didn't, and she felt anxious.

The door across the room opened. A guard stepped in, followed by a man wearing an orange jumpsuit.

"Thirty minutes," the guard said, closing the door behind him.

A man of medium build stood 10 feet away from her. He had short, dark hair. He was clean-shaven, with no apparent tattoos. She looked for cuffs on his hands or feet but saw none.

"My name is Rick," he said, stepping toward her and extending his hand.

"Hello, I'm Michelle," she said, rising to her feet and taking his hand.

His palm and the inside of his fingers were soft.

"May I sit down?" he asked.

"Of course," she said, motioning to the other chair.

"Thank you, Michelle," he said.

They sat down, facing each other. Michelle wasn't sure what to say. Just then, she remembered the reason she was there and the bag of cookies on her lap.

"Here," she said, handing him the cookies. "These are for you."

"Thank you," he said, taking the bag.

He looked down at the bag, checking out the cookies inside.

"Do you mind if I try one?" he asked.

"Not at all," she smiled. "They're for you."

He unzipped the plastic bag, reached in and pulled out a cookie.

"Would you like one?" he asked.

"No, thanks."

He bit into a cookie.

"Mmmm," he said. "Delicious. I've had these before."

"No, I don't think you have," she said. "I baked them myself, and this is the first time I've baked cookies for this program."

"No," he said, munching. "I've had these cookies before.

Chocolate chips, peanut butter and M&Ms. In fact, I've requested them—from Mrs. Rigby."

"You have?"

"Yes, she told me a woman named Anna baked them."

Michelle's heart skipped a beat. She swallowed.

"Pardon me?" she said.

"I don't know her last name, but I've been her biggest fan here for the past couple of years," he said.

"I made those cookies according to a recipe my mother taught me when I was a little girl," she said.

"Is your mother's name Anna?"

"It was."

"Was?"

"Yes. She passed away a couple of months ago."

"I'm sorry."

"Thank you."

"I guess that explains why I haven't had these cookies in a while."

He looked at her.

"I'm sorry," he said. "That sounds so selfish. I didn't mean it that way."

"I know," she said. "It's okay."

"Do you mind if I have another?" he asked.

"Go right ahead."

He bit into the second cookie.

"So you're probably wondering what I'm in for," he said.

"Yes, I was curious," she said.

"Embezzlement."

"How long is your sentence?" she asked.

"Three years."

"How much do you have left to serve?"

"Five months, four days and 20 hours," he said. "Give or take."

"Congratulations in advance."

"I hope I make it," he said.

"Why wouldn't you make it? Are you in danger?"

"Not from the other prisoners," he said.

"What then?"

He looked over toward the mirror.

"You know that's a two-way mirror, don't you?" he asked.

"I figured it was."

"Do you know what it's like to be watched all the time?"

"No," she said. "No, I don't."

"Well, it makes you feel like you're always under suspicion, like you can't be trusted. After a while, it takes the life out of you."

Michelle could see the pain in his face.

"Do you have a family?" she asked.

"Yes," he said. "I have a wife, Emily, and a daughter, Sophia."

"They trust you, don't they?"

"What do you mean?" he said, sounding irritated.

"I mean your wife and your daughter know you well. They know you not as a prisoner, but as a husband and a father."

"Yeah," he said. "I guess they trust me."

"I'm sure they do, and I'm sure they love you."

He looked down and didn't say anything.

"How often do you get to see them?"

"Once a month," he said.

"And in a little more than five months, you'll get to see them every day."

"Yeah," he said.

His face was expressionless.

"You must be looking forward to that," she said.

"My daughter's eight years old," he said. "I've been in prison for most of her life. She's hardly knows me."

"You mean this isn't your first offense?" she asked.

"No. It's my second. I got 18 months the first time I was convicted of embezzlement. I've screwed up my life. I've screwed up my family's life. I wouldn't blame them if they left me."

"They're not going to leave you, Rick."

"How do you know that? You don't know anything about me."

"You're right," Michelle said. "But I know your wife has stayed with you all this time and that she and your daughter come to see you whenever they can. They must love you."

"If you say so," he said, sounding defeated.

Michelle sat there, unsure what to say.

"Do you write them letters, Rick?" she asked.

"Sometimes," he said. "Why do you ask?"

"I don't know. Nobody writes letters any more. I mean real letters. I used to write letters to my friends and my cousins when I was a girl, and they wrote me back. Do you know I still keep those letters under my bed? There's something about letter writing. I don't know—it connects us. When you get a letter from someone, in their own hand, well, you feel a bond, that's all. It changes you, and you realize you're not alone, that there's somebody out there who cares about you."

There was a knock at the door. It opened. The guard stepped in.

"Time," he said.

Rick was looking at Michelle. He was on the edge of his seat, leaning in, as if he were hanging on the last thing she had said.

"Let's go," said the guard.

Rick and Michelle stood up.

"It was a pleasure meeting you, Rick," she said, extending her hand.

"It was a pleasure meeting you, Michelle," he said. "Thank you for the cookies and the conversation. I'm sorry for your loss."

When Michelle got home, her father had already left for the airport for a business trip. She poured herself a glass of red wine and heated some leftover pasta and had dinner in the kitchen.

She thought about her conversation with Rick. She thought about what she had told him about writing letters. She thought about the old letters under her bed.

She finished dinner, put her plate in the sink and walked down the hall to her bedroom. She got down on her knees and looked under her bed.

She was expecting to see the cardboard box she had always kept there. Instead, she saw only a flat, opaque, plastic bin. She grabbed it and pulled it out from under the bed.

She snapped open the latches on both ends and pulled off the lid. Inside were all her old letters, arranged in neat stacks. *Mom must have done this*, she thought.

There was an open space on the left end of the bin. There, resting on the bottom, was an envelope which simply said *Michelle*. She would have known that handwriting anywhere. It was her mother's.

She sat down on the floor. She could feel her heart racing. With shaking hands, she reached down and picked up the envelope. She ran her forefinger under the flap, breaking the seal. Inside were two sheets of paper, folded in thirds. She pulled them out, unfolded them and read the handwritten letter.

February 16, 2006

Dear Michelle,
I hope this letter finds you well.

I hope you won't mind that I transferred your old letters to this plastic bin. Your old cardboard box was starting to fall apart, and I thought this bin would keep your letters safe.

You have been such a joy in my life. I have always felt so close to you. By the time you read this letter, I will have passed on. But not really for I will always be with you.

I am sorry your first job out of school didn't work out, but I am proud of you for walking away from a job in social work which didn't allow you to connect with people.

Connecting with people is what life is about, and it has always made you happy. I know you will find new ways to connect with people and, as you do, you will be fulfilled. That is my prayer for you.

Thank you for all you have done for me, especially during my illness. Being with you, not just these past months but all your life, has been the greatest joy I have ever known.

I put this letter here, with all your other letters, because I know how much corresponding with your friends and cousins meant to you when you were a girl. These letters might seem dated now, but the connections you made, the pathways you opened, are timeless, and their impact is beyond measure.

I hope you will always connect with others,

Michelle. Let people know they are loved. It is your gift and your highest purpose.
I love you.
Mom

Michelle sat there, holding her mother's letter, and wept. She cried a long time.

Then she got up, stepped over to her desk and sat down. She turned on the desk lamp. She slid open the middle drawer and pulled out a sheet of white paper, then plucked a pen out of the coffee mug on the desktop. She placed the paper on the black, leather desk pad and began to write.

May 16, 2006

Dear Rick,
Do not despair ...

Blessing

Presence

Jacob's fifth-grade classmates were thinking about him when he wasn't in school after his mother died, but they didn't know how or even whether to reach out.

Jacob had always been a "mama's boy." Now, without his mother, he felt so alone.

One day after school his friend Chloe came over. She lived a few doors down.

"Jake!" his father called upstairs. "Chloe's here for you."

She was standing in the foyer when he came down.

"Hi," she said.

"Hi," he said.

Neither of them knew quite what else to say and, at 11, hugging seemed too awkward.

"Want to swing?" she asked.

"Okay," he said.

She followed him into his backyard. They walked through the grass to his swing set and slipped into the yellow rubber swings, as they had countless times as children. When they were small, their mothers pushed them on these swings.

"Higher!" they would scream, laughing with delight and holding on tight. "Higher!"

Now they said nothing. They simply glided back and forth, like pendulums. Jacob felt as though he were suspended between two worlds, the one he had known and some other world where he would never feel his mother's loving touch again.

After a few minutes, Jacob slowed to a stop and Chloe did too. He stood up, shading his eyes from the late afternoon sun and hiding his tears.

A mourning dove flew in low overhead. It landed gracefully on the peak of the swing set and perched there.

"I love you" was the last thing Jacob's mother had said to him. Then she closed her eyes, and she never opened them again. He wondered if her words might still be in the air, hovering like a spirit above her bed.

"I need to go in," he said.

"Okay," said Chloe.

He started walking back to his house. She followed him, then veered into the side yard to let herself out through a wooden gate, as she had many times before.

Jacob stopped on his patio and looked over at her. Chloe was his oldest friend. He had known her long before his mother died, and he hoped he would know her long after. That idea, her coming over that afternoon, her being at the gate just then gave him comfort.

"Thanks," he said.

"Take care," she said.

Stay

Ben had fought in a "forever war" for 20 years when the US finally pulled out. He had passed up nearly two dozen chances to end his tour and go home. Not that he cared for the conflict. He stayed because he incurred a great debt in that faraway land and he felt duty-bound to repay it.

Ben was an only child, the son of an abusive father and a mother he couldn't remember. She vanished when he was three. No one knew why.

For the next two years, Ben had a host of "mothers," women who also lived in the trailer park. They kept an eye on Ben while his father was at work. On average, that was about three days a week. For Ben, those were the good days, when he was beyond his father's reach.

The surrogate mothering stopped, though, when Ben turned five and started kindergarten.

"If you're old enough to go school, you're old enough to fend for yourself," his father said.

Ben took a bus to and from school. Some mornings, his father was still asleep when Ben left. When Ben got home, his father was usually gone or passed out.

That was the routine all through grade school. By the time he was in high school, Ben started drinking. One night, he came home drunk, and his father cursed at him. Ben cursed back. His father came at him, but Ben, who was now as tall as his father, slugged him in the jaw and knocked him out. After that, Ben's father never laid a hand on him again.

On his eighteenth birthday, Ben enlisted in the Army. He took a train to Fort Benning in Georgia. His father didn't even say goodbye. Ben spent 10 weeks in basic training, then shipped out to Afghanistan.

Maybe Ben didn't hear the command. Or maybe it was because he wasn't used to being on defense. Or maybe it was just be- cause he was still green. But he got separated from his unit, which came under attack in a small town.

Ben huddled behind a stone wall near a small house. Peeking over, he saw a group of soldiers advancing up the hill. For a moment, he was tempted to fire down on them. But then he remembered he was alone and realized that would be suicide.

"In here," said a small voice behind him.

Ben wheeled around. A small girl stood in the doorway of the house. A man and a woman stared out from behind her. "Hide in here," the girl said.

Ben heard gunfire. It was coming from the town, from others in his unit, he suspected. Then he heard the soldiers just below returning fire. They were getting closer.

He knew he had to find cover. He didn't know what might lay waiting inside the house, but he was willing to risk it. Staying low, he made a break for the open door.

When he was inside, the girl shut the door behind him. Ben looked around, his rifle still at the ready. The girl who had let him in had backed up against the man, who put his arms around her. A small boy, smaller than the girl, stood with his back to the woman.

The man said something in Pashto, which Ben didn't understand. The girl looked up at the man and said something in Pashto too. He looked at her and nodded.

"Hide here," she said to Ben, stepping quickly to the middle of the room.

The man and woman followed her. They grabbed opposite ends of a rug and slid it across the wooden floor, revealing a small trap door. The man pulled back the door, looked up at Ben and pointed down.

"Hide here," the girl said.

Ben stepped over to the opening in the floor and looked

down into it. He could see a ladder but nothing beyond that. Outside the sound of gunfire was growing louder. Realizing he had no other choice, Ben climbed down the ladder until he reached a dirt floor. Someone closed the trap door above him, leaving him standing in total darkness.

He heard footsteps above and the rug being dragged across the floor. He heard chairs being scooted, then low talking, then silence.

He heard a door swing open hard, then men's voices. They were all speaking in Pashto, their voices rising. Heavy footsteps thundered around the room above him. He heard chairs being scooted again.

Then he heard a man yelling. Then another man yelling. Then gunfire and screams. Then thuds. Then no more screams. Then heavy footsteps. Then men's voices. Then a door creak

open. Then voices trailing off. Then nothing.

Ben waited in the cool darkness for what seemed like a long

time, his heart pounding, until he was sure the soldiers were gone.

He climbed the ladder and slowly pushed the trap door up slightly. He peered out but could see nothing because the rug was covering the door. He pushed the door open all the way, but the rug still covered it. He made his way up the ladder and pushed the rug aside.

He looked around and saw the bodies of the man, the woman and the children lying on the floor, blood seeping out from beneath them.

The door was open. He stepped over to it, gripping his rifle. He looked around. Seeing no one, he shut the door.

He went to the woman and knelt beside her. No pulse. Then the man. No pulse. Then the boy. No pulse. Then the girl. When he put his fingers on her neck, she moved slightly and moaned.

She was covered with blood. He slung his rifle over his shoulder and scooped her up. She opened her eyes and cried out.

"It's okay," he said. "I've got you."

He managed to open the door while holding the girl, then went out to find his unit.

Her name was Sadia. She was eight years old. During her operation at a field hospital, Ben waited, nervously pacing outside. Between maneuvers, he visited her there during her long recovery.

Without her father, mother and brother, Sadia had no one. So Ben sort of adopted her. He managed to stay near her and care for her throughout his first tour. Then he re-upped so he could continue to care for her.

He fed her, clothed her and gave her shelter. She called him Papa and gave him her heart.

Through the years, Ben watched Sadia grow up. He watched

her fall in love and get married. He watched her have children and care for them lovingly. Sadia taught them to call him Papa too. He became their Papa, and they became his family.

It was a most unorthodox arrangement. But Ben's commanding officers knew the back story. They always cut him slack, and for 20 years he was a reliable pair of boots on the ground.

When the US decided to pull its troops out of Afghanistan, Ben was torn. Should he go home or stay in the place which had become his home?

"Stay with us, Papa," Sadia said.

He looked at her and thought of the first time he'd seen her.

"Hide here," she said. They had saved one another. But not just that. Because of her, he became the father he had never known. Because of him, she became the mother he could not remember.

Ben was honorably discharged. He handed in his rifle, gathered in his family and stayed.

Together

John and Christine met in their twenties in a shoe store in Manhattan. From the moment their fingers touched over a single shoe, they knew they were destined to be together.

A year later, they pledged their lives to one another. Ten years later, still childless and weary of the big city, they decided to start fresh. For years, they had dreamed of Alaska. Now they ventured there by train to make a new home.

They had a cabin built on the shore of Auke Bay. From their front porch, they watched glaciers calving, great frozen endpoints, once liquid, breaking free and returning to their origin.

For 40 years, they lived there simply, quietly and happily. They both taught at the local campus of the University of Alaska until they retired. They were inseparable.

Then one November, Christine became ill, very ill. John brought her to doctors in Juneau, but they could do nothing for her, so he brought her home.

As the snow began to fall, John cared for Christine day and night, but she grew ever weaker. For each of them, the thought of losing the other was nearly unbearable. In their suffering, they were fused.

In the spring, a neighbor went to their cabin to check on them, but they weren't there. Then he discovered a single set of deep footprints in the soft soil from their front steps to the water's edge.

Saved

The homes in my neighborhood were built 50 years ago. Only one of the original residents still lives there. His name is Bill Harper. He lives three doors down.

Bill lives alone. His wife died last year. Until recently, I hadn't met him.

I don't know most of my neighbors. Until the pandemic, I wasn't home much. I'm in sales, and I used to travel four days a week. But with everyone hunkering down and hardly anyone flying, I've been working from home.

It's been strange. Before, I set up appointments and called on customers. Now I live on Zoom.

It's been a big adjustment. Not just the work. But where I work and even where I live. I feel like a stranger in my own house. My wife and kids are driving me crazy. They're noisy, and they're always interrupting me. I lock the door to my office upstairs, but they still manage to get in. Some days, I can't get anything done.

Lately, I've been taking walks just to get away. It's quiet in the neighborhood. With the pandemic, everyone's inside. I like that. No need for small talk.

A few weeks ago, I went out for a walk. I was walking by Bill Harper's house when I heard someone call, "Good morning."

I looked over and saw Bill sitting on his front porch. He was wearing pajamas and reading the newspaper.

"Good morning," I said. "Beautiful day."

"Yes, it is."

I smiled, gave him a little wave and kept walking. I'd almost passed his driveway when he called, "Got a minute?"

I didn't want to be rude, so I stopped.

"Sure," I said.

"I've got a quick question, if you don't mind."

So much for my quiet walk, I thought.

I walked up his driveway. Bill got up and laid the newspaper down. He was tall and thin. I knew he was old. I'd seen him, driving by his house, many times. Now, close up, he looked even older. His face was drawn, and his pajamas hung on him like a farmer's clothes on a scarecrow.

As I approached, he pulled a face mask out of his pocket and put it on.

"Just to be safe," he said.

"Oh, yeah," I said, pulling my mask out and slipping it on.

We stood there, two masked strangers, looking at each other for an awkward moment. I wondered what he wanted.

"I'm sorry to bother you," he said. "Do you know how to use Zoom?"

"Yeah."

"Well, Carol has — had — a computer, but I really don't know how to use it. I was wondering ..."

"Would you like me to show you how to use Zoom?"

"Yes. But if now's not a good time ..."

"Now is fine."

"Oh, good. Please come in. By the way, I'm Bill Harper."

I climbed the two steps to his porch and gave him a gentle fist bump.

"I'm Matt. Matt Jenkins. I live a few doors down."

"It's good to meet you, Matt. I know you're busy. I won't take but a minute of your time."

He turned around and pushed open his front door. I noticed this took some effort.

"Come in," he said.

I followed him into the foyer.

"It's right here," he said, shuffling into the dining room. Near the edge of the table was a laptop, a MacBook Air. It was open. A power cord dangled from the computer to a wall outlet. The morning sun through the windows filled the room with bright light. Looking around, I noticed a layer of dust on everything.

Bill pressed a button on the keyboard, and the screen lit up.

"I never turn it off. I'm afraid I won't be able to turn it back on. I don't know Carol's password."

"I see. Do you mind if I sit down?"

"Please," he said. "Would you like something to drink? Some coffee?"

"No, thanks."

He pulled out a chair at the end of the table and sat down too.

"I'd sit next to you, but, you know," he said.

"I understand. Do you happen to have a Zoom account?"

"No."

I set one up for him.

"I need to show you how to use it. Why don't you sit here?" I said, patting the seat of the chair next to me. It's okay. We're wearing masks."

Bill pulled out the chair and sat down beside me. He folded his hands in front of him on the table. I noticed they were trembling.

I showed him how to set up a Zoom meeting.

"Do you happen to know who you'll be meeting with?" I asked.

"Yes. My children and my grandchildren, I hope. I haven't seen them since before the pandemic."

"Have they come to visit?"

"No. They think it's too risky for me."

"I'm sorry. Well, now you should be able to see them." "Thank you."

He was staring at the computer. I noticed his eyes were moist.

"Is there anything else I can help you with?"

"No," he said, getting up. "You've been most helpful."

I followed him to the front door. I stepped ahead and pulled it open.

"I can't thank you enough, Matt."

"You're very welcome, Bill. It was good to finally meet you."

I started to give him a fist bump, but he opened his arms and embraced me. Standing back, I saw tears in his eyes.

"Are you okay?"

"Yes," he said, wiping his eyes.

I wanted to know for sure he was all right but didn't want to embarrass him. So I wished him a good day and invited him to call me with any questions.

I walked back down the driveway and took off my mask. I had gone for a walk that morning to be alone. Now solitude seemed so lonely.

I decided not to continue my walk. I went home.

A Day in My Garage

One Saturday morning, I was working in my garage when I felt funny and had to sit down. As I looked around, my son's dusty bike in the corner caught my eye. Then somehow it was no longer his bike, but mine when I was a kid. And I was standing next to it, and my father was standing next to me.

The last time I'd seen my father, he was in his casket. But now he was not only alive but young. I had no memory of him looking so youthful. And I was a boy of seven or eight.

We used to work on my bike a lot. When we did, my father was always in charge. "Watch," he used to say. It was his way of letting me know he was going to show me how to do something and do it right.

Of course, even as a boy, I knew what he meant. I wasn't capable. He never came right out and said that, but I got it. Growing up, whenever I was around my father, I felt inferior, especially when it came to anything mechanical.

Around tools, he definitely knew what he was doing. He could just look at a bolt and know the exact wrench for it. Using wire cutters, he would strip off the coating without ever clipping the wires. When he sawed a board, his mark was exact, and his cut was flawless.

Saying we worked together on anything was really a misnomer. *He* worked, and I watched. He seldom let me do anything. He was the master, and I was his apprentice, and it was best for me to simply observe.

Now, standing next to my old bike, the task before us was to attach a new headlight and electric horn to my handlebars. They'd come in a white cardboard box, which I vaguely remembered was a birthday gift.

My father opened the box and pulled out the bulky silver headlight. A long, plastic-coated wire dangled from it. At the end of the wire was a silver clasp sporting a black button, for the horn.

My father pointed out where everything would go. Then, holding the light where my handlebars met the steering column of my bike, he did something he'd never done before. Instead of getting to work, he just stood there and said, "Go ahead."

It took me a moment to figure out what to do. I wasn't used to thinking on my own. I looked at the headlight and saw it had two metal clasps beneath it. Each had two screws with small, square nuts. I realized the screws would need to be removed and the clasps attached to my handlebars, so I grabbed a screwdriver and a wrench.

While my father held the light, I inserted the blade of the screwdriver into one of the screw heads and tried to loosen the nut with the wrench, but it was too big. I expected my father to tell me which wrench was right or grab it himself. But he just stood there, holding the light, saying nothing.

Feeling anxious, I stepped over to his workbench and picked out a smaller wrench. This one worked. Slowly, I removed the nuts. Then, with my father's help, I attached the light to my handlebars and tightened the clamps.

"Good job," he said.

I couldn't believe it! He'd never paid me a compliment.

I then went about attaching the clasp for the horn. Again, at first, I picked the wrong wrench. But then I found the right one and secured the clasp. My father watched in silence.

Now the light and button for my horn were in place, but the wire that connected them hung loose, drooping over my front tire. I looked at it, unsure what to do, and thought for a moment.

"Should we tape it?" I said.

"Good idea."

I realized that the wire was so long that it would need to be wrapped around my handlebar. For that, I would need to loosen the clasp for the horn and wrap it along with the wire around my handlebar.

That was a two-man job, so my father and I worked together. He held the wire down as I wrapped a roll of black electrical tape around and around, covering my right handlebar.

The whole time, my father said nothing. As I turned my new light on and off and beeped the horn, he stood back and watched, with a small smile on his face.

My father was stoic. He said little and was stingy with praise. But transported back to that moment, reliving an experience I had long forgotten, I sensed my father was proud of me.

I looked up at him and said something I don't recall ever saying to him until he lay dying.

"I love you."

His eyebrows arched. He looked startled. Had I gone too far?

But then he said, "And I love you."

My eyes moist, I blinked, and I was back in my garage. I looked around, hoping I might catch one more glimpse of my father, but he was gone.

Trust

Jennifer Mattson was more than 20 years older than Josh Parker when she began to fall for him. She was 48, and he was just 27.

It was not a physical thing at first, although he did stand out simply because he was older than all the other students in her freshman English class. He was also well dressed, unlike her other students, who wore sweatshirts and jeans. But the main thing that attracted Jennifer to Josh was his unique combination of self-confidence and vulnerability.

During the first class of the semester, as everyone introduced themselves, he said, "I'm Josh Parker. I'm 27, so I guess I'm the old man in this class. I went to work right after I graduated from high school. I have a good job. I'm selling commercial time for WBZ radio and making good money. But I know my future's going to be limited without a college education. So I've decided to go to school while I'm working. I know it's going to take me a while to get my degree, but I don't mind. When I'm a CEO one day, it'll be worth it."

It was that blend of humility and bravado that got Jennifer's attention.

At first, Josh wasn't a very good student. His grammar, spelling and overall writing skills needed a lot of work. He was behind most of the other students in the class, and Jennifer didn't want to slow them down by going over the basics with everyone. So she offered to tutor Josh.

"Thank you," he said, smiling. "I'd love that."

"Great," she said. "Can you stay after class once in a while?"

"No, I can't. I'm sorry. I need to get back to work right after class. Can we make it some other time?"

They quickly concluded that, given their schedules, meeting during the day wasn't going to work.

"Well, I'd be glad to meet you at a restaurant or, if you like, host you at my house," Jennifer said.

Even as she said that, she was concerned that her offer might seem too forward or possibly inappropriate, but Josh didn't seem to mind.

"I doubt we could get the privacy we need in a restaurant," he said. "I'd be glad to come to your place."

Josh said this with such earnestness, even innocence, that Jennifer said, "Okay. How about this Friday evening?"

"That would be great," Josh said. "Where do you live?"

Josh wasn't married, and Jennifer had been divorced for more than five years. She didn't date much, and so the idea of having a man in her house was a big deal, even if it was a student.

Housekeeping wasn't one of Jennifer's strengths, even though her kids were now out of the house and she lived alone. Knowing Josh would be coming over this Friday, she spent time each night that week cleaning every room on the first floor. She also got her nails done and her hair cut and colored.

———

Josh arrived at 7:00, right on time. He was wearing jeans, a black golf shirt and brown suede shoes.

"Hello, Josh. Thanks for coming over."

"Good evening, Professor. Thanks for hosting me."

Stepping inside and looking around, he said, "Wow! You have a beautiful home."

"Why, thank you, Josh. May I offer you something to drink?"

"No, thanks. I just had dinner."

"Okay. I thought we could work in the dining room. That's where I usually do my work. There's plenty of space there."

"Sounds good, Professor. Lead the way."

"It's right in here," she said, motioning with her left hand.

She started to walk ahead of him, then stopped and turned around.

"Josh, if you're comfortable, I want you to know it's okay to call me Jennifer, at least when we're not in the classroom."

"Okay, Jennifer," he said with a smile.

Hearing him say her first name gave her a warm feeling inside and made her ears tingle.

As they sat down at the dining room table, she got a whiff of his cologne. It smelled earthy. He pulled a few of his recent papers from a handsome, black folder and put them on the table.

"I had some questions on some of your edits and comments on these papers," he said. "I thought we might start there."

"Certainly," she said.

She then proceeded to go through all of her comments. He listened closely and seemed to understand.

He then asked if he could share a draft of his latest assignment, a three-page paper, for her input before he finished it.

"I'd be glad to,"

"Thank you, Jennifer," Josh said.

Again, she had a warm feeling inside when he said her name. This time, her whole head, not just her ears, tingled.

He slid his paper over to her.

"May I write on this?" she asked.

"Please do," he said.

As he slid his paper across the table, she noticed the sinewy muscles in his forearm and felt her heart beat faster. She slipped her glasses back on and began to read it.

As she read, she could feel his eyes upon her. She looked up several times, and he was indeed looking at her. Instead of looking away, though, he just smiled. She noticed how straight and white his teeth were.

She made notes on his paper for about 15 minutes.

"All right, Josh. I've got some comments and suggestions for you. But let me say first that this is a very good start."

"Thanks, Jennifer. And let me say I really appreciate how positive and constructive you are. I wish more of my teachers were like you."

Now her whole body was tingling.

She scooted her chair closer to his and slid his paper over until it was almost in front of him. He scooted his chair toward hers. Now only a leg of the table separated them.

She went over her comments slowly. After most of them, Josh said, "Got it." But after some, he said, "I'm not sure I understand." That vulnerability again. She was only too glad to explain further.

When they were finished with his pending assignment, he thanked her and put all his papers back in his folder.

"Anything else I can help you with?" she asked.

"No, I think that'll do it."

"May I offer you anything before you go?"

Hmmm, she thought. *That didn't sound right.*

"No, thanks," he said. "I've taken enough of your time. I'm sure you have things to do on a Friday night."

I wish I did, she thought.

"And I'm sure you have things to do too," she said.

"Not really," he said. "It's a quiet night for me."

"Me too."

"Well, it's really quiet in your house. Isn't anybody else home?"

"No. I live alone."

"Oh," he said, his eyes widening, as if he was realizing this for the first time.

He got up, and she got up too.

"Josh, I really appreciate the extra effort you're making in our class," she said, walking him to the front door.

"And I really appreciate the time you've spent with me this evening, Jennifer."

"Anytime."

"Really? I might take you up on that."

"I hope you do."

She opened the front door, but before he stepped out, Josh turned to Jennifer and gave her a hug. His body was lean and firm and felt so good.

He let her go and said, "Good night."

"Good night," she said. "I'll see you in class on Monday."

She watched him walk away and wished she could have held him a little longer.

The next morning, Jennifer went to the gym to work out. Afterwards, she stopped at the market for groceries. Then she went home to grade papers and get ready for her classes in the coming week. Of course, that made her think of Josh. Sitting at her dining room table, she closed her eyes and took a deep breath through her nostrils. She could still smell a trace of his cologne in the air.

It was past 6:00. She was hungry but not eager to make dinner, so she went out to a favorite restaurant nearby. It was a warm and pleasant evening, and she sat on the patio. Over the years, she had learned to dine alone without feeling self-conscious, though she never learned to like it.

She spotted an older man and a younger woman a couple of tables over. They were having drinks and sharing an appetizer. He was laughing and seemed to be doing most of the talking. All the while, he kept leaning in toward the young woman.

At one point, he reached across the table and rested his hand near her plate, as if he expected her to take it. Instead, she sat back in her chair, looking uneasy. He said something to her, and she got up, Jennifer assumed, to go to bathroom. The man sat back in his chair, looking unhappy, and motioned to the waitress for the check. As soon as the young woman returned, he got up, and they left.

The next day, Jennifer got a call from her daughter Sarah. She often called on Sundays just to catch up. Sarah said she was fine, but from her tone of voice, Jennifer sensed that wasn't the case.

"Honey, is everything okay?" she asked.

"I'm okay, Mom," she said. "But it's been a tough week."

Sarah told her that a few days earlier, she had to file a complaint with HR because her manager had begun coming on to her.

"At first, I didn't believe it," she said. "I mean he was such a great boss. He really helped me, and I trusted him. But when he began to flirt with me, I knew I could no longer work for him because I could no longer trust him."

They talked for a while longer. Jennifer thanked Sarah for sharing what had happened and told her she was proud of how she had handled it.

"Thanks, Mom," she said. "Sometimes it's hard to know who to trust. I'm glad I always have you."

The next day at school, Josh showed up for English class. When he walked in the classroom, he smiled at Jennifer, and she smiled at him.

He stayed after class to talk with her.

"Thank you again for helping me last Friday," he said.

"It was my pleasure."

"I was wondering if we might do it again this Friday—if you're free, of course."

She looked at him, as if for the first time, as if she did not know his name, only that he was one of her new students. She tried to put aside her feelings for him and see him as he was: a young man trying to get his college degree and depending on her to develop skills he would need to succeed professionally. Then she remembered the young woman in the restaurant and thought about Sarah.

"Josh," she said, "I wish I could, but I can't. I really want to help you. I'm happy to help you. But from now on, if I do that, it has to be either here in the classroom or in my office. I hope you understand."

"Of course, I do, Professor," he said, looking a little relieved.

They met several more times that semester in Jennifer's office, always with her door open. She always came prepared with helpful comments and suggestions on his writing. He listened carefully and continued to improve.

Ultimately, Josh earned a B in the class. It took him seven more years to get his undergraduate degree in business. During that time, he got married, and at 40, he became a CEO.

To Be a Saint

"Welcome, saint," Saint Peter said, greeting heaven's newest member.

"Saint?" said the newly disembodied soul.

"Yes," he said with a smile. "Well, you will be soon enough. Congratulations."

"Thanks," said the soul, looking around. "Am I in ..."

"Yes," said the old man. "You made it."

The soul smiled. Well, to the extent a spirit can smile.

"Wow," said the soul. "I'm not sure what I did to deserve this, but I'm grateful."

"Don't be so modest. You were a paragon of virtue on Earth. Not only that, you performed miracles."

"I did?"

"Yes, at least two. That's why you'll be canonized."

"You're kidding."

"I don't kid."

"Oh."

"Let's see," Peter said, pulling out a device.

"Is that the new iPhone 16?"

"Pro Max," Peter said, tapping the screen. "Now what was your name?"

"Jack. Jack Samuelson."

"Short for John?"

"No, just Jack."

"Interesting," Peter said, brushing his index finger across the screen. "Oh, yes. Our records show you kept countless people from starving and prevented a man from taking his own life."

"Really?"

"Don't you remember?"

"Yes, I do. It's just that ..."

"What?"

"That wasn't me."

"What do you mean? Your name was Jack Samuelson, wasn't it?"

"Yes, but I wouldn't have done those things if it hadn't been for Bill Jacobs."

Peter leaned on his staff and shifted his weight. Looking tired, he again swiped his screen.

"William Jacobs?" he said.

"I guess so. We all called him Bill."

"From Kansas City?"

"That's right."

"Jacobs joined us 30 years ago," Peter said. "Apparently, he got in by the skin of his teeth."

He looked up at Jack.

"Don't repeat that."

"I won't."

"He died in prison," Peter said.

"Well, that's where I met him. He was serving a life sentence for armed robbery."

"You were in prison?"

"Yeah, when I was young."

"Why?"

"Larceny."

"Really? How long were you in there?"

"Eighteen months."

"I see. And that's where you met Jacobs?"

"Yeah, he was my cellmate."

"Well, he must have done something right because he's up here now."

"Bill did a lot of good for a lot of people."

"Like what?"

"Well, for starters, he set me straight. Growing up, I thought the world owed me. That's why I started stealing things. I'd convinced myself I was entitled to other people's property."

"And Jacobs set you straight?"

"Yeah. He was the first person who ever really listened to me. Up to that point, everyone had pretty much ignored me. When I met Bill, I felt worthless. I really didn't care about myself or anyone else for that matter. I think Bill sensed that. He told me, 'You are the light of the world.' He told me I could make the world a better place, but only if I cared about both others and myself."

"And did you do that?"

"Yes."

"How?"

"When I got out and got a job, I remembered what Bill had told me. When I got my first paycheck, I gave half of it to Feed the Children. I wasn't making much money then, and I almost couldn't believe I was giving half of it away. But it felt right."

"And you kept doing that?"

"Yeah, I gave away half the money I ever made. Not always to

Feed the Children. But always to some charity that fed hungry people."

"Well done," Peter said. "And what about the guy who was going to kill himself?"

"I met him on a plane. He was sitting next to me. It was a long flight, and we started talking, sharing our stories. After I told him I'd done time, he opened up and told me he struggled with depression. He even told me he'd attempted suicide. Next time, he said, he'd be successful."

"And what did you do?"

"I told him what Bill had told me. 'You are the light of the world.' At first, he laughed. But then I told him how thinking of myself that way and helping others had changed my life. He seemed stunned. He started crying. He looked out the window and didn't say much for the rest of the flight. But when we got off, he thanked me and gave me a big hug."

"Did you ever see him again?"

"No. I always wondered what happened to him."

"He became a motivation speaker," Peter said, squinting at his screen.

"Really?"

"Yes. He gave the most popular TED talk of all time. He credited you with saving his life."

"You're kidding."

"I don't kid."

"Oh, yeah."

Peter stared at Jack as if he were looking through him. Actually, he *was* looking through him.

"So you're telling me if it hadn't been for Bill Jacobs, you wouldn't have performed those miracles?"

"I'm telling you, if it hadn't been for Bill, I wouldn't be here."

"I see," Peter said, slipping his iPhone through a slit in his cloak. "Well, we're glad you're here, John — I mean, Jack. Again, welcome."

Then he pointed to a pearly gate just a few feet away.

"There's the entrance," he said. "If you'll just step inside, I think you'll be very happy with all that awaits you."

"Thank you," said Jack.

Then he pulled open the gate and stepped into eternity.

As the gate swung closed, Peter reflected on his conversation with Jack as well as his conversations with two other newly admitted souls earlier that day. They too were slated for canonization.

He realized they all had something in common: their extraordinary lives were made possible by others who, behind the scenes, had shaped and even saved them, ordinary people who had now blended into the heavenly crowd and weren't up for sainthood.

Peter stroked his long, white beard. Time to talk with The Big Guy, he said to himself. We need to rethink what it means to be a saint.

Listen

Clara awoke in the near darkness. She strained her ears but could hear nothing. She peeled back her covers, got out of bed and stepped carefully down the hallway, touching the plaster wall with her fingertips to guide her way.

She reached a doorway and went in. A nightlight cast a faint glow about the nursery. Clara went over to the crib and leaned down to get a close look at her infant son. He appeared to be sleeping. She stared at his face and chest, eager to see him breathe. He stirred, and she breathed a sigh of relief.

She reached down, smoothed his hair and held the side of his face in her hand. Then she went back to bed and slept for another hour before she woke up and did the same thing again.

For the first two years of her life, Clara had the hearing of a normal child. But just before her third birthday, she contracted meningitis.

It nearly killed her. Over many months, her health was restored, but she lost most of her hearing.

It was a time before most people, especially children, wore hearing aids. Clara went to school with the other kids, but there was no special education for children with disabilities. Nearly deaf, she had a hard time keeping up and was labeled a "slow learner."

Clara was 16 before she graduated from the eighth grade. School had been so difficult and frustrating that she decided not to go to high school. Instead, she got a job selling men's clothing in a local department store.

One day, she met Henry there. He had just graduated from high school and come in to buy a suit, as he had just accepted a sales position with a local paper company. Clara was taken by his smile and careful way of speaking. She could read his lips. It was as if he knew about her.

She asked Henry what type of suit he was looking for and showed him the store's offerings. As she described the various styles, he listened to her carefully and watched her closely. She had never had a man pay so much attention to her. She liked that.

She helped Henry pick out a suit and a shirt and tie to match, and a tailor took his measurements. Clara walked past the open entrance to the fitting room and saw Henry standing on a wooden platform, with the tailor on his knees, marking the hem of his pants. She didn't mean to stare, but Henry looked so handsome in his brown, double-breasted suit. He spotted her in the trifold mirror and smiled. She blushed and hurried back to the cash register, but she was glad she had seen him that way.

Before he left the store that day, Henry introduced himself to Clara. He extended his hand, and she took it. Something felt so right to her about holding his hand.

He came back a week later to pick up his new suit. Clara knew when it would be ready and made sure she was working that day. Seeing Henry again made her feel warm inside and a little dizzy.

As she rung up his order, Henry asked Clara if she would like to have dinner. She could hardly believe he had asked that and thought she might have misheard him.

"Pardon me?" she said.

"I said would you like to have dinner sometime?"

"I would love to," she said, smiling.

A year later, Clara and Henry were married, and a year after that, their first child, a boy, was born.

———

Henry was a wonderful husband and a doting father. He also happened to be a very heavy sleeper, and he seldom woke up at night when his children were babies. Getting up with the children at night was a role Clara would play.

Over 15 years, they had seven children. When each of them was a baby, Clara woke up nearly every hour at night to check on her newborn. She couldn't hear if they were crying, and she had to be sure they were all right.

She would examine them closely in their crib to make sure they were breathing. Sometimes, they would be crying, and she would pick them up and hold them, feed them, sing to them. Sometimes, she would pick them up even if they were sleeping just to hold them and watch them fall asleep again in her arms.

Even when her children were no longer infants, Clara would check on them at night. Thus, as everyone else in the house was asleep, Clara was tiptoeing from room to room, keeping watch over her children.

As a result, she got precious little sleep herself. Over time, this took a toll on her. She aged rapidly. At 25, Clara looked 40. When she turned 30, her hair was turning gray, and her face was wrinkled.

Henry grew concerned. He begged Clara to get more rest, but she always waved him off.

"I'm okay," she would say, "and I have to know our children are okay too."

By her mid-40s, Clara began forgetting things. She developed tremors, and her speech became soft and slurred.

Henry insisted she see a doctor. Finally, she gave in. Tests showed she had Parkinson's Disease and dementia.

After that, her decline was rapid and steep. By the time she was 50, Clara was bedridden. Her doctor said there was little more he could do for her. He mentioned a nursing home, but Clara insisted on staying in her own home and implored Henry to keep her there.

"Of course," he said, holding her hand.

Her need for care was nearly constant now. Henry was still working, so each of their children, all of them now adults, took turns caring for their mother. They each took one day of the week. It was a full day too because they always got up at night to check on her.

At last, Clara's body forgot how to swallow. For two days and two nights, Henry and all the children gathered around her. They were all with her the morning she took her final breath.

It is said that God hears every leaf that falls in the forest. If that's true, it must be because every leaf is dear to him and he listens with his heart.

Carousel

I found myself standing on a spinning carousel, holding onto a twisted brass pole. A panoply of images encircled me, people and experiences from throughout my life.

I watched them all pass by: every friend and enemy, every success and failure, every joy and sorrow. They all blended together.

I wanted to stop and behold the miracle of my daughter being born. I wanted to unsee my mother dying. But I couldn't stop or close my eyes or pick and choose.

It was all my life, every part indispensable, and as I looked around and held on tight, I felt grateful for the whole of it.

Acknowledgments

I want to express my appreciation to the following people for their helpful feedback on various stories: my wife Liz, Kathy Kennedy, Patti Normile, Libby Belle, John Young, Christine des Garennes, Anna Gayford, Murray Bodo, Christine Sneed and Nina Bailey.

I also want to thank Farrukh Kahn for his cover design and Beth Anderson and Jon Virgi for their expert formatting.

Finally, I want to extend grateful acknowledgement to the editors of the literary magazines where the original versions of some of these stories first appeared: *Literary Yard, Friday Flash Fiction, Scarlet Leaf Review, Bright Flash Literary Review, Red Fez, Flash Fiction Magazine* and *Scars Publications*.

About the Author

Don Tassone is the author of two novels, one novella, one children's book and 10 short story collections. He and his wife Liz live in Loveland, Ohio. They have four children and 12 grandchildren.

9 798218 651138